Dr. Do-Right
A best friend's brother, off-limits romance
Julia Fisher

Contents

Dedication   V

Trigger warnings   VI

1. Chapter 1   1

2. Chapter 2   11

3. Chapter 3   26

4. Chapter 4   35

5. Chapter 5   47

6. Chapter 6   59

7. Chapter 7   69

8. Chapter 8   84

9. Chapter 9   101

10. Chapter 10   118

11. Chapter 11   129

12. Chapter 12   144

13. Chapter 13   158

14. Chapter 14   166

15. Chapter 15   180

Epilogue   194

Also by Julia Fisher   206

About the author   208

Acknowledgements   209

To anyone who was told they were "too much."

I'm sorry the people around you weren't enough.

Trigger warnings

Chapter 1

Happy birthday, Kitten.
Surprise!

I stared down at the note in my hands. The masculine, angular script was as familiar as my own. I could probably forge it, if I really wanted to. The words were cryptic, though. What surprise? This package was the least surprising thing to happen to me today. It had been delivered right on time, like clockwork.

"So, did we decide on how many twinkle lights is too many? Like, what's the line between disco and desperate?" Sonia's voice traveled down the hallway, coming closer. My heart leaped into my throat.

I spared one glance at the note and the box it had been delivered with: a sleek, black package containing what looked to be a truly spectacular silver vibrator. I shoved both hastily behind the purple velvet chair in my room, spinning to check myself in the mirror as the door opened. *Whew.*

"Because I won't lie. I want to do more," Sonia continued as she breezed in, platinum hair perched in curlers on her head.

She had her gold under-eye masks on and was wearing an old, paper-thin sleep shirt that showed off her generous curves. Somehow, even with Medusa hair and blobs on her face, she was too beautiful to seem real. Her face was all angular features and sharp green eyes that still intimidated the hell out of me when she got pissed off.

A sharp stab of guilt prickled my gut. *Don't look at the box.* I swallowed the uncomfortable feeling down.

"It's my birthday, Sonnie. More is more." I checked myself one last time in the mirror, trying to calm my heart rate. It had been pounding ever since I'd seen the plain brown package sitting innocuously on our counter, which meant Sonia had gotten it from the mail room before I'd had a chance to grab it.

My reflection, at least, looked more collected than I felt. I'd worked some magic on my usually unruly hair, the dark, nearly black strands falling in big bouncy waves around my shoulders. Black liner and purple shadow emphasized my brown eyes.

"That's what I was thinking, but I am getting seriously concerned about blowing a fuse." Sonia glanced suspiciously at the walls.

"We were fine when we rented that bounce house for Thanksgiving last year," I reminded her, moving to my small walk-in closet.

Clothes hung haphazardly off hangers. My mother would have a coronary if she saw it, but she'd never even graced my apartment building with her presence, so I tried not to worry about that too much.

My outfit, thankfully, had been picked out for days: cream silk bustier with a stretchy black mini skirt. The issue, though, was the shoes. Wasn't that always the issue?

On one hand, my purple Louboutins made my legs look miles long and would make my outfit pop. On the other hand, we were planning a rager. Did I really want to be teetering around on 6 inches after a few margaritas?

Did I really want to vamp it up when the one person I wanted to look good for wouldn't even be here?

"That's true. And at least with the lights, we don't have to move all the furniture." Sonia paused for a moment. I could hear the gears turning all the way from the closet. "I'm gonna go for more lights."

"Wait! Before you leave. What do you think?" I presented the Louboutins and a pair of sparkly flip-flops for her consideration. She didn't hesitate to tap the purple patent leather.

"The red bottoms, obviously. It's your birthday, and I specifically told everyone to bring cool, single dudes." She clasped my shoulder, leaning in closer to stare into my soul. "This dry spell of yours has gone on for too long, friend. Time to get laid."

"Ha!" My fake laugh was a little too loud. I sounded like an enraged donkey. "We'll see. You know work has been just... bonkers."

It was a weak excuse, even if it was true. I was a nurse practitioner in the cardiothoracic surgery unit at Cedar Hospital, so intense pressure was pretty much always the name of the game. Between sprinkling in a new class of residents and the mentoring initiative I'd taken on, the free space in my brain quickly filled.

But even when it was hectic, nursing was a good gig. I worked long shifts, but it meant I had a few days off a week, and most nights. There wasn't *really* a reason for my dating life to have dried up like it had. At least, not a reason Sonia could know about.

I kept my gaze on hers, forcing myself not to look at the purple chair.

"Too bad Mal couldn't make it tonight. He always loosens you up." She brushed a curl of hair off my shoulder.

Do not look at the chair. Seriously.

I tugged my heels on, casting an eye around my room to avoid her. There was a small wrinkle in my emerald green duvet cover. I pulled it smooth. "He'll be here later this week," I responded, looking at everything but Sonia.

"He told me he had a surprise for us." She tilted her head this way and that in the mirror, giving her best duck face. "I'm thinking a red lip tonight. What do you think?"

"A surprise?" That word, the note...

Happy birthday, Kitten. Surprise!

What game was he playing, and why was he involving Sonia? It was very, very against the rules. I reached into my makeup drawer for my tube of NARS lipstick in her favorite red shade. I needed to do something with my hands.

She rolled her eyes when she plucked it from my fingers. "No clue. You know how dramatic my brother can be. Maybe he's flying us to Cancun? Maybe he got us a new blender to replace the one he broke last month? Who knows?"

Do. Not. Look. At. The. Chair.

I huffed, mindful not to bray a laugh like before. "Let's hope for Cancun."

"For sure. Okay, I'm going in for more twinkle lights. If I go quiet in there, I've been electrocuted."

"I'll come help you in a sec!"

My sigh of relief was on the tip of my tongue, but she whirled around before she got to the hall.

"Did you see that package from earlier? Birthday present?"

In my imagination, the box behind the chair suddenly poofed into flames while neon arrows blinked and a giant sign unfurled, reading, *"Look at me! I'm a secret box!"*

I suppressed the audible gulp that rose in my throat. "Nah, it was just some shampoo I ordered from an Instagram ad a few days ago. Nothing fun."

"Ooh! That new viral one with the green tea? Can I try it?"

"Duh." I made a mental note to order a bottle on rush delivery when I got the chance. The longer this charade continued, the harder it was getting. This wasn't the first time Sonia had innocently questioned one of Malachi's little deliveries. It probably wouldn't be the last.

"Unless you end it with him. Put both of you out of your misery. Stop lying to your best friend," a little voice inside my head whispered. I accepted the wave of guilt that washed over me. I never hid anything from Sonia, ever. Except this.

After six months, I still wasn't used to the unease slithering around my belly. I felt torn in two, half of me rushing after Malachi, the other half clinging to Sonia, my best friend in the whole world. From the rift in the middle, guilt surged, bubbling over to trap me like a fly in sticky, inescapable fear.

I couldn't lose her, but I knew I'd always regret it if I lost him. I was caught in between them and unable to make a decision either way.

I carefully placed the Louboutin bag in my closet as she walked away to find more lights. A silent sigh gusted out of me. I listened to her footsteps, making sure she was all the way in the living room before I grabbed the note and the box. I clutched them to my chest, fingertips brushing across the edge of the cardstock.

He'd held this in his hands. Thought of me while he penned it.

Ugh. I was ridiculous. That still didn't stop me from carefully placing the note and box underneath the Louboutin bag on my shelf. I folded the cloth over reverently. I'd come back for it tonight.

Later, lights hung, guests arriving any minute, Sonia clicked her glass against mine.

"To my bestie. Long may she reign."

"Here, here! What am I the queen of, again?" I took a sip, the lime and tequila hitting just right.

"Amazingness. Badassery. Looking hot." She grinned when I snorted, looking me up and down. "This is, by the way. Very hot. Boiling. 'Project get Rija laid' is definitely a go."

I glanced down at my clothes. I'd picked them out when I'd thought a certain someone would be attending my party. But celebrity business has a tendency to pop up unexpectedly. I understood why he'd had to bail, but now I wished I'd worn something more casual. I wondered if it was too late to go grab those flip-flops, or if changing my shoes would make Sonia suspicious.

After all, I was supposedly wholeheartedly bought into this getting laid plan.

"It's been a while for you. Do we need to go over the rules?" Sonia leaned against our kitchen counter. It was gleaming white. Sleek. Just waiting to get buried in bottles and Solo cups and lime wedges.

"Ah, yes. Don't mix liquors after midnight. Always use protection. Code word is papaya if some dude is getting too weird and clingy. And...of course..." A burr stuck in my throat. "Hands off your brother."

"Memory like a steel trap, this one." Sonia applauded while I hid my grimace with another taste of margarita. Right on cue, a knock sounded at the door. "Dry spell ends tonight, baby!" She grinned, swinging open the door to reveal a handful of our nursing school friends. The first in an endless wave of partiers who would help me ring in a new year of life.

I fixed my smile on my face, running through the rules again in my head, repeating the only one I'd ever had trouble with.

No mixing after midnight.
Use protection
Code word is papaya.
Hands off Malachi.
Hands off Malachi.
Hands off Malachi.

***

It was after midnight. I had not mixed liquors, and I'd used papaya three times.

Sonia glared as she walked number three over to the karaoke machine, having rescued me from the most boring conversation known to man. There was only so much I wanted to hear about cryptocurrency.

She thought I was being too picky. She wasn't wrong. I had very specific tastes in men these days.

Tall, dark, and untouchable pretty much summed it up.

I stopped to chat with people on the way to the kitchen, accepting all the hugs and happy birthday wishes my little heart could handle. After a few drinks, I was on the tipsy side of buzzy. My wits were still about me, but I was loose and warm and happy, surrounded by all the people who loved me. Well, most of them.

I was chatting with one of Sonia's friends from the hospital when a shrieky gasp cut through the apartment. I'd know that shrieky gasp anywhere. Sonia was excited about something.

"Ri! RiRi!" she yelled. I left my glass on the counter, grinning while I yelled back, our voices carrying over the thumping sound system.

"I'm coming, I'm coming! Please tell me you hired a stripper."

"Not my day job, but I'll make an exception for the birthday girl." That voice stopped me in my tracks. Low, lilting, humming with barely suppressed laughter. My favorite sound in the world.

I gasped, staring at Dr. Malachi Dobrev as he walked through my front door. "I thought... I thought you had work?"

"*Surprise,*" he whispered in my ear, pulling me in for a tight hug. My arms wrapped around him on instinct, pulling him even closer. His belt buckle dug into my belly.

"Isn't that the famous TikTok guy? The therapist?" someone muttered behind me. But I was focused on another, more pressing question.

"What are you doing here?" My voice was muffled by his shoulder. He still hadn't let go. I didn't either. He felt too good, all of him pressing against all of me. The type of contact we rarely had. I savored it.

"You don't think I'd let something as stupid as work keep me from my favorite girl on her birthday?" He finally pulled away, eyes roaming across my face, cataloging it like we'd been apart for years, even though I'd just seen him last month. "Don't tell Sonia I said that," he whispered, tucking a strand of hair behind my ear. It dragged through my lip gloss. His eyes followed.

"Ri, look what he brought you!" Sonia was doing the shrieky thing again. A flash of a resigned smile crossed his face.

"It's not for you. He's for me. But you can hang out with him if you want." Mal stepped backwards to take something out of Sonia's arms. Standing like that, close to the door, in travel-rumpled clothes, he looked so much like the night I'd met him, it sent an aching throb through my chest.

That silky dark hair. Teasing smirk. It was all the same now as it had been that night two years ago.

Except this time, he held a squirming puppy in his hands.

"Happy birthday, Rija."

Chapter 2

Two years earlier

I had prepared for this, I really had.

When Sonia had told me her brother was the social-media-famous Dr. Do-Right, you could have knocked me over with a feather. I couldn't have been more surprised if she'd informed me she was related to Air Bud.

"This guy? That guy? Is your brother?" I shoved my phone in her face. I'd pulled up his channel, clicking on a random video with a few million views.

"Yes! That's my brother, Malachi."

"This...*this man?*" I watched as he laughed at something an interviewer said, gesturing with his hands as he discussed tips for maintaining intimacy in long-term relationships.

"Yes! That is my brother."

"Y-you...look nothing alike!" It was the only thing that came to my mind, other than, *oh, God, her brother is hot.*

"We're both adopted, Carrie," she droned, referencing a truly dimwitted woman from our nursing program. We'd taken to calling each other by her name when we did or said particularly dumb shit. It wasn't often, thankfully.

"I know but... I just don't get why you didn't say anything till now?"

I'd known she had a brother, of course. I'd known her for four years, lived with her for three. She had a mom and a dad and a brother, all of whom still lived in Colorado. She dutifully flew to see them on major holidays. I'd waved to her parents on FaceTime before, but, come to think of it, she always took calls from her brother in another room. Sus.

"Exactly because of this." She snatched the phone away, shutting the video off. "Listen, I've been told that he's hot." She pretended to gag. "Sometime around high school, I realized all my friends were, like, totally gaga over him, which is gross. Once I got to college, whenever he visited or met my friends, it was like they fell under his spell."

I frowned, eyeing my phone. It wasn't beneath her to unlock it and set my home screen to a picture of her butt, or something. I'd have to grab it back soon. "Well, that sucks, but it doesn't—"

She held up a finger. "I'm not done. Christine, my roommate freshman year? Wouldn't stop asking me to set them up. She followed us to dinner one night when he was in town. Literally stalked him. Still texts me sometimes about him."

"Okay, that's crazy, but—"

"Naomi, my high school friend, always wanted to hang out when I went back home from college, but ditched me constantly to hang out with him instead."

I winced, starting to get the picture. "Yikes."

"He actually dated my friend Jess, just before I met you. It was bad. So bad. When he dumped her, she barged into my biology class and started screaming at me. She was my best friend, and she totally lost her shit over him."

"Fuck, Sonnie, I'm so sorry." I rubbed my thumb across her hand. That sucked. Big. My bestie talked a big, loud, confident game, but I knew she was more sensitive than she let on. Her friends and her family were her entire world. Having so many of them abandon her for her brother must have been horrible. My heart broke a little for her. "Why didn't you ever tell me?"

She sighed. "I was scared. You're like my BFF soulmate, Rija. I couldn't stand to lose you, too."

"Hun." I pulled her up from her chair into a hug. "You'll never lose me. You're my best friend."

"He's coming into town this weekend, and he wants to see my apartment. And meet you. I'm fine with it, now, but...Rija you have to promise."

"I promise." I said, without needing to clarify what the promise was. Sonnie was my soul sister, more family to me than my actual family was. Whatever she needed, I'd make it happen.

"I'm serious. Please, just...stay away from my brother. Hands off, you know?"

"Sonnie. I swear. I will not touch your brother. Now give me my phone back."

I was familiar with Dr. Do-Right. *Malachi*. A couple's and family counselor who'd ridden the social media wave to become one of the most famous therapists in the world. Like, celebrity status. I wouldn't say he was Dr. Phil or anything, but he wasn't far off, and it was easy to tell why.

Besides promoting his feel-good platform of doing right by other people and yourself, the man oozed sex appeal, especially when he was dishing out scintillating bedroom advice and winking at the camera. Despite his rising popularity, he still managed to keep an air of humility about him. Top the whole package off with his doctoral degree from Yale and legitimate counseling chops? Consider my panties practically dropped.

But no longer. I was shutting down that train of thought before it left the station.

I did my research in preparation for his visit. Watched his videos—all of them, even the ones from a few years ago with bad lighting. I'd acclimated to his deep-set, piercing black eyes. Those high cheekbones and the Romanesque nose, covered in smooth, olive skin. Dark swaths of hair that hung nearly down to his chin.

I'd even cranked the audio, inoculating myself against his smooth, intellectual timbre as I listened to his closing tagline again and again, "Remember, if you're going to do anything, try and do right."

I'd thought I was prepared.

I was wrong.

Nothing can prepare you for Dr. Malachi Dobrev. Not when he's standing in front of you, in the flesh.

"Rija. You're the one keeping my little sis in line, huh? I'm Malachi."

His dark eyes sparkled with mischief as he stood in our entryway, framed by the front door. His fingers were warm as they wrapped around mine. Nearly hot, like vitality was leaking out of his pores. His teeth were straight. Shiny. I wanted to know what they'd feel like sinking into my skin.

I blinked, trying to remember all my preparations and mantras. Alas, the only thought running through my head was that Malachi Dobrev was the hottest man I'd ever met in my life.

Somehow, against all odds, he was more attractive off-camera than he was on my phone screen. One look at him set my heart racing. My skin tingled where it touched his. Goosebumps shivered up my arm. The sharpening of his gaze told me he knew it, too.

And was interested. His lips curled up in a sinful smile.

I'd done the only thing I could do: jerked my hand away, glared at him like he'd tracked poop onto the carpet, and run away.

I'd managed to avoid him for the rest of the night. His visit coincided with me and Sonia's truly epic annual Cinco de Mayo party. The apartment was packed with plenty of people to buffer the charged air between Malachi and me. I ruthlessly placed as many bodies between us as possible.

Sure, his relationship advice was sound and always evidence-based. And his family counseling center in Colorado was literally raking in awards and charitable grants to support his work with under-represented populations, and families and couples who couldn't afford traditional counseling.

But that didn't matter. Over the years, too many people had chosen him over Sonia, and I refused to be another one of them.

I had resolved to be polite, but distant. To not give the man a second glance after he walked in the door that night. All that resolve had crumbled to dust the second he'd wrapped his hand around mine. It continued to flail like one of those car lot blow-up men as he seemed to chase me around the party. I couldn't get away from him, no matter how hard I tried.

Eventually, I escaped to the blessedly quiet kitchen, rinsing a few glasses to get a jump on tomorrow's dishes.

"I can't help but notice you're not avoiding anyone *else* at this party. So, I have to assume I've done something to upset you." Even though I'd only known him for an hour, I could still identify his voice over the pounding bass and chattering voices beyond the kitchen. *Dammit.* "Which is odd, since I just met you earlier tonight and you've barely said a word to me since."

"I'm not avoiding you." I was, but I didn't have to admit that to him. I shot a haughty glare over my shoulder. "Like you said, we just met. How conceited do you have to be to assume I'm thinking anything about you, at all?"

I was thinking *everything* about him. I'd thought I'd been prepared. I was so unprepared. I was like a toddler in an OR. No clue what I was doing and surrounded by potentially dangerous, pointy objects. I couldn't keep my eyes off him, no matter how hard I tried. He'd cast his freaky voodoo on me, and I didn't know what to do about it other than to act unforgivably rude and then sprint in the opposite direction.

"No, you've definitely been avoiding me. Impressive, considering how small this place is. I almost hopped over the couch earlier to catch you when you were talking to the redhead."

I steeled my spine and turned around to face him. Bad move. One look and I was drowning all over again. No wonder so many of Sonia's friends had gone down like the Titanic. He smiled when I turned, like I'd done it just for him, and he liked that.

"I think you mean *Nurse Daley,*" I over-emphasized her credentials. "She's a very intelligent, capable woman who is more than just her hair color."

Maybe he was a misogynist? Honestly, it would make my life easier. *Come on, Dobrev. Give me something to hate you for so I can slam the door on this crazy lust swelling inside me.*

"Joanna *is* very intelligent and capable. I was just talking to her about her campaign to include more LGBTQ+ representation in the clinical trials she's assisting. She and her partner are doing great work at the shelter downtown. We had a good chat about it. You should have stuck around."

"I know about the work they're doing at the shelter," I snapped. I'd accompanied Joanna and her girlfriend, Maggie, several times, giving free medical exams and updating prescriptions for LGBTQ+ teens who had been kicked out of the house or were down on their luck. The fact that he'd so quickly learned about the work that was so close to their hearts seemed like a point in his favor. *Dammit.*

"Maybe I'll see you around, then. I've offered to hook them up with some counselors I know in the area. Do a video on the shelter to boost visibility. It's good shit."

It *was* good shit, and another point in his favor. Or maybe like five points, given how casually he'd offered his help to mere strangers at a party, just because they were doing meaningful work.

I scowled, officially enraged by selfless acts.

"Again, I have to ask: are you this frosty to everyone? Or is the honor all mine?" He circled around the small kitchen island, setting off a fresh wave of panic. I could barely clench my fingers around the crazy attraction I felt for this guy. If he came any closer, it was going to start dropping out the sides, like an overly-full pile of laundry.

My panties would be at his feet.

"I'm inclined to think it's just me. Sonia talks about you like you hung the damn moon. And you've been perfectly lovely to everyone else here. I have theories, of course." He smirked, reaching around me to pull a bottle of tequila closer.

I'd snagged it in hopes of making myself a drink strong enough to douse whatever mating instincts were making me want to leap across the room and run my tongue over his lips. As he pulled back, his forearm brushed against mine. Just like when he'd shaken my hand, sparks erupted where we touched. Sweat prickled my neck.

His eyes flicked down to the point of contact, eyebrow quirking before he met my gaze again. "That's theory number one."

"I don't know what you're talking about." I sounded strangled. Probably because I was simultaneously trying to hold my breath to avoid breathing him in, and attempting to take deep soothing inhales to calm down my nervous system. A challenge, sure, but I was very capable. Most of the time.

He smelled like the ocean.

"I think you do, but I'll spell it out for you, if you'd like." He filled a plastic shot glass and slid it in my direction, reaching across the counter for a lime and some salt. "You don't strike me as the type that needs much spelled out, though. Maybe you've just forgotten what crazy sex hormones feel like. Nursing is a stressful profession. I can't imagine you have much time for dating."

Was it just me, or did that question sound hopeful? Very leading. He was fishing to see if I had a boyfriend. I didn't, but admitting that felt like conceding another point and I was already woefully behind on the scoreboard.

He continued when I didn't respond. "If we're going down the 'spelling out' route, I'll tell you that I'm very, very attracted to you and I'd like to explore that further, if you'd also like to. I think you would, considering how your pupils dilate every time you look at me."

Oh, fuck. I liked the way he was so candid about...everything. Leave it to a world-renowned therapist to lay everything out there without a trace of ambiguity.

He held up a finger. "Sorry, I misspoke. Very, very, very attracted to you."

"Was that a necessary point of clarification?" I rasped, watching as he set the limes and the salt in easy reach.

"Just making sure we're on the same page. Something in here's telling me we would be very, very, very good together." He rubbed his knuckles back and forth across his chest.

Instead of running his eyes down my body when he talked about how good we'd be together, he focused on my face. Weirdly, it was hotter that he looked into my eyes when he said it. Like he was truly seeing me and not just my body, and *that* was what attracted him. *Me.*

Impossible, of course, since I'd given him the cold shoulder all night. Right. Cold shoulder. That's what I was supposed to be doing.

But he'd stepped just close enough that my personal bubble rubbed up against his. Like a cat looking for pets. Well, my personal bubble might be ready to roll over and give it up for him, but I was not.

"You have nothing to offer me I couldn't accomplish with my vibrator." I'd meant for it to sound derogatory, but somehow it ended up sounding like a challenge. Or an invitation.

Interest flared in his eyes, so I backtracked hard. "I'm serious. I'm not interested. I refuse to be one more of Sonia's friends sacrificed to your dick."

The light in his eyes died, giving way to a serious, confused frown. "Sacrificed to... Okay, I admit the thing with Jess was a bad idea. Like, cataclysmically bad. But I swear, I have never touched one of Sonnie's friends before or since. That was five years ago.

I thought she said she was over that." He glanced down at the counter, rubbing his jaw.

"Well, she's not. And it's not just Jess. Do you know how many friends she's had to stop hanging out with because they were just using her to get to you?"

He stared at me for a beat, his face falling before he cleared his throat and stepped away to a more respectable distance. My bubble was intact once more.

"I did not know that. Thank you for telling me." He seemed...contrite. And sincere, like he really was glad to know this information, and not defensive or offended like I'd expected him to be. "I wish I'd heard it from Sonia, herself. I'll talk to her about it later."

That, again, was a truth I hadn't expected. My family was more of the *have a massive blow-out then sweep it under the rug* type. Maybe Malachi Dobrev actually was the real deal, practicing what he preached through his channel.

"I...well, yes. You should."

He glanced at me, side-eyed. "If I promise not to sleep with you, will you hang out with me? Or are you going to pretend I have leprosy for the next week?"

Dammit. That's right. Not only did I have to survive this party, but Malachi was visiting Chicago for an entire week, crashing at a nearby hotel. I was sure to see him around again.

I sighed, looking at the shot in front of me. It was better than looking at Malachi. Every time I did, I noticed something else: the freckle on the tip of his nose, slightly off-center and extremely kissable. Or the way he ran his fingers through his hair, smoothing it back subconsciously.

"I'll hang out with you," I conceded. A little drawbridge over the freezing moat that was currently protecting my reproductive system.

Regardless of Sonia's friends' unfortunate history of falling for her brother, she loved him fiercely. They'd stayed close as they'd grown up. Whenever he was in town, I hardly ever saw her. It would be good to actually get to hang out with her this week, now that I'd met him.

It had taken her several years, but now she finally felt comfortable letting me into their lives. I didn't want to push the opportunity away. I knew how important both he and I were to her.

"You don't even have to bring the vibrator. Though, admittedly, we could have some fun with that." He scrubbed his palms over his face, grimacing like he was in physical pain. Everything south of my belly button clenched at the idea of having some fun with him and my vibrator.

"Careful, Doctor Dobrev."

"Yes, ma'am. Sorry." He sighed, his breath smelling like mint and limes. I wondered if he tasted that way, too.

He held up his shot glass, and I clinked mine to his. Both of us tapped them on the table before downing them, as if we'd done it a million times before.

Despite my growing attraction over the next week, we kept the flirting to a minimum. After he'd gone back to Colorado, a plain, brown-wrapped package had showed up at my door. The first vibrator he'd ever bought me, shaped like a little green cactus. The note had said, "For the best Cinco de Mayo I've ever had. Even if it started out a bit prickly."

The note and the gift had made me smile. We'd laughed about it a few months later when he was back in town (outside of Sonia's earshot, of course. We hadn't technically done anything wrong, but by unspoken agreement, we kept this particular inside joke quiet.).

The next Christmas, a little candy cane vibrator. His next trip in town was around Valentine's day. I got a little pink Rocket. On and on. The packages showed up, we laughed about it later, and in the meantime, I got myself off thinking about him.

Also, in the meantime, he and Sonia and I became closer than I could have imagined. We laughed until our sides hurt over chips and salsa. I learned about the work he was doing at his clinic and through social media. How he wanted to make sure that all families had resources to get help, even if they couldn't afford traditional counseling. He asked me poignant, probing questions and, surprise, surprise, was a great fucking listener.

Month after month, visit after visit, as the three of us got closer and closer as a unit, the strings connecting me to Malachi also pulled taut. Until they snapped.

Sonia had been working the late shift one night while Mal was in town. One too many margaritas found us slouched on my sofa, ignoring the Parks and Rec episode playing in the background.

"What's the theme for this visit going to be?" I wondered out loud, attention snared by the buttons he'd opened at the top of his shirt. As always, the tension simmered between us. By unspoken agreement, we kept a tight lid on it when Sonia was around. Now she wasn't here, and it was spilling over.

"I've always wondered, do you use them?" He pulled on his lower lip while he studied me, eyes at half mast. The sight of him reclined across the cushions made my blood run hotter. I was in over my head.

"Yes," I whispered the truth. We'd been circling around each other for just long enough, and my inhibitions were just low enough, that I wanted to set more of that scalding chemistry free. I was tired of ignoring it, even though I knew why we had to.

A low grunt punched out of him. The raw desire on his face made me look away. My eyes flickered down, only to settle on the bulge at the front of his pants. *Ah, fuck, that wasn't any better.*

"You like them?" He murmured, gaze raking down my body. My nipples puckered against the lace of my bra.

"Yes."

His tongue darted out to wet his lips. They gleamed in the low light of the TV. "Good."

We kept staring at each other, chests rising and falling too fast for two people just sitting on the couch. I swallowed, reminding myself again and again: *Don't touch Malachi. Don't touch Malachi. Just touch yourself later.*

Like a coiled spring, the thought set off a chain reaction that shook me all the way to my core. A realization. I couldn't touch him. But I could touch myself.

"Would you like to see?" I didn't recognize my voice, so husky and low. He studied me for a second, downing the rest of his drink.

"Fuck, yes."

I didn't touch him at all when he watched me take myself to orgasm twice with my favorite toy. And I didn't touch him when he jerked off as he watched.

The rest, as they say, is history.

Chapter 3

Present day

"I can't believe you got me a puppy," I repeated for the hundredth time, grinning down at the dog in my arms.

"Sigmund is *my dog*. If you just so happen to want to walk him and sleep with him and play with him when you're not at work, I'll allow it." He smiled softly, watching me rub the puppy's lopsided ears.

Malachi had been doing a promotional video for an animal shelter and apparently hadn't been able to leave the puppy behind. As someone who'd always wanted a dog and could never have one, I was in heaven when he curled up in my lap, placing his chin on my chest.

Mal might say Siggy was his, but we both knew the truth. This wiggly little fur ball was mine, especially since both of them were planning to stick around.

"I can't believe you're moving to Chicago," I murmured, careful not to disturb the puppy.

"I can't believe she went to bed over an hour ago and you still haven't spread those thighs for me."

I glared at Malachi, eyes flicking to Sonnie's door. It was the wee dark hours of the night. Not a creature was stirring, besides me, Siggy, and Dr. Do-Right. Still, better safe than sorry. "Shh. It's almost like you want her to hear."

"Oh no. That would be horrible," he intoned, sarcasm dripping from his words. If Mal'd had his way, Sonia would have known about our *activities* months ago. I sighed.

The movement made the puppy wiggle. Mal's eyes darted to the dog, jealousy darkening his face. I added insult to injury, smooching Sigmund's scruffy little nose and rubbing under his chin while his tail whipped back and forth. "We're going to be neighbors, aren't we little one? Are we going to be best friends? Are you my best friend?"

Mal had planned several surprises tonight, beginning with him flying in after his work meeting, and ending with him breaking the news that he was moving to Chicago. He'd even managed to snag the penthouse unit in our apartment building, so he'd be close while he opened up his new counseling center in the city. I was still reeling at the news, both terrified and thrilled with its implications.

As usual, Mal could read me like a book. "We should talk about what this means for us."

"I'm hoping it means you'll figure out some better storage solutions. My bedside drawers are both already full."

I'd thought a few times about clearing them out. Maybe purging some toys he'd bought me over the last two years that didn't quite get me there. But I ran into a few problems every time I considered it. First, what does one even do with used sex toys? Was there some sort of recycling program out there?

Second, as weird as it sounds, I was pretty sentimental about most of them. The little orange one, for instance, had been a gift for the first time I'd completed rounds on my own as an NP. It didn't do the trick, but it made me smile to think about how he'd gone out of his way to same-day ship it so that it would be waiting for me when I got home that night. And how he'd set his alarm from...I think he'd been in India at the time?...to FaceTime me to ask about how my day went. And then watch.

So, that's where I was. Just a girl, stuffing increasingly large volumes of sex toys in my drawers and praying my best friend never found out. There was a metaphor in there somewhere. Probably because one day, the drawer would get too full—the secret too big—and they'd all come springing out to slap her in the face with my betrayal.

"Kitten, you can have a whole dresser. At my place."

I avoided his gaze, running my fingers across the dog's fur. He was so snuggly, I wanted to die. "Careful, Doc."

"I don't want to be careful, Ri. You know why I'm doing this."

"Because your Colorado location is going to bust at the seams soon. And you love this city. And your sister is here, who you adore."

He sat forward, propping his elbows on his knees and fixing me with that perceptive stare I both loved and hated. He loomed in the chair on the other side of the coffee table. I'd sprawled on the couch, the table a strategic, unspoken barrier to keep ourselves from jumping each other.

I could see his beautiful brain working overtime, analyzing the situation, my reactions, the best way to meet me there. Usually, I loved watching him work, but sometimes when he turned those perceptive therapist eyes on me, I wanted to cringe away.

"My biz dev team could make the same cost/benefit analysis for a clinic in New York. But I do love Chicago. In part, because my sister is here." *In part because* you *are here.* We both knew the words hung there, unspoken, between us.

Just like we both knew why I was cuddled up with a dog right now. Why he'd showed up to my birthday with a puppy, when the last time I'd seen him, we'd discussed how I'd always wanted a dog growing up. How that yearning had never changed and how much I regretted that my work schedule wouldn't allow me to care for a pet.

Some people might think a puppy was an over-the-top gift from a long-distance, no-touching fuck buddy, but it really wasn't.

In the past six months, even though we now had a physical outlet for all the need we felt for each other, our explosive chemistry hadn't fizzled. Instead, our attachment had grown. Those guilty little sessions behind closed doors with my vibrator had turned into long-distance video calls that went for hours into the night.

Within that time, there were more reasons than ever for Mal to be in Chicago. Long weekends after conferences or a client meeting he couldn't take over video call. Flimsy excuses to stay at our apartment instead of a hotel. More dinners, lunches, drinks, walks around the lake, laughter, and good times with the Dobrevs than I could count.

Sonia loved that he was around more often. She'd gleefully renamed our group chat the Three Musketeers. At first, I could pretend we were just three really close friends, and I wasn't in love with one of the other musketeers, and that he didn't regularly feed my sex toy habit, or watch me climax.

But six months into keeping this secret with him and we were both wearing thin. The hot, illicit feeling of watching each other come had shifted from "I bet you feel so good" to "I want to touch you so badly" to "I would give anything to put my hands on you" and now we were floating somewhere in a bittersweet longing.

The more I saw of Mal, the more I wanted to see of him, and not just in a hot, naked way. The thrill of it all had worn off. Now, I didn't just want him in bed, but everywhere. I wanted him to be mine, fully. The feeling had grown stronger in the last few months, but I didn't know how to address it.

Sonia had been a pivotal force in my life since the day we met, anchoring me when I was unmoored. She never accused me of being *too much*, despite what my family had told me over and over again. She taught me not to take life too seriously. That I was worthy of love, even if I was loud, sometimes.

At the same time, Malachi's steady, thoughtful presence and single-minded insistence that I deserved what I wanted (even if was getting myself off in front of my best friend's brother) had made me bold in other areas of my life, too. He read my mind when I was overwhelmed or reeling from some family drama. He made me laugh and turned me on more than should be physically possible.

I wasn't sure I could make it in this world without both of them. So, I'd just maintained this awful little secret, feelings of love and guilt growing in equal measure, trying to figure out when the other shoe would drop.

Apparently, the shoe was dropping right into the penthouse seven floors above me.

"Ri, it's been months. Surely she'd understand."

"She'd understand that we've been lying right to her face this whole time?"

Mal sighed, staring at where the puppy had fallen asleep in the crook of my arm. "I don't want to hurt her. But I also don't want to do this anymore."

"What do you want, Malachi?" I whispered, even though I already knew the answer. Like me, he was tired of hiding, tired of the tortuous restrictions I'd placed on us. I was at my limit, and apparently, he was at his, too.

"I want to take you on a date, Rija. And actually kiss you. And keep fifty drawers for you at my place." He looked pained, dropping his head into his hands. "I want to know what your nipples taste like."

I knew he saved that final, whiny confession for last just to get a laugh out of me. He succeeded. "Poor thing."

"You have no idea."

I did. "Mal." I only hesitated a second before reaching over to lace my fingers with his. We both sucked in breaths at the contact.

We'd decided early on that hands didn't count. We couldn't avoid fist-bumps and high-fives forever. Still, we reserved any hand action for serious or extra-special occasions. Discussing the future of our relationship seemed like both.

He cupped his other hand around mine, trapping my fingers between his palms. His skin was warm. "Please, Rija. I'm moving to Chicago for you. I won't pretend differently. Meet me in the middle, here."

No beating around the bush for Dr. Dobrev. His determined chocolate eyes and quiet plea pulled at something in my chest. Unraveled it. I braced myself for the fear. I should have been terrified, considering exposing our secret to my best friend. Instead, relief bloomed in my chest. He'd be here, finally, after so many years of only having part of his time. I wanted all of his time, all of him.

He was right. It had been long enough. I was tired of keeping secrets, and exhausted from loving him so fiercely and still not knowing what his lips felt like on mine.

"Okay."

His forehead dropped to where our hands joined. A relieved sigh ghosted over my knuckles. I felt it echo in my bones. "You're sure? I need you to be sure."

"Mal, I'm miserable. The thought of telling Sonia about us makes me want to puke, but..." I trailed off when his eyes met mine. Yes, the thought of hurting Sonnie made me physically ill, but the thought of keeping Malachi at a distance was killing me. I owed it to him, to me, to explore what this could become. I owed it to Sonia to stop lying to her. "You're right. We need to tell her."

He heaved another sigh, light breaking across his face. "Yes. Let's tell her."

"Just..." My gaze flicked to her door.

He groaned, resting his cheek on our hands. "Rijaaaaa. Don't make my year just to bring me back down again."

"No more rules or secrets, I swear. Let's just...hold off on anything until we tell her."

"You're saying I can't fuck you tonight." He looked at me like I'd just kicked the puppy in my arms.

"I haven't broken my promise to her yet. I know it's all semantics. I know, I know, I know. But not touching you is the only thing keeping me from being a truly horrible friend. At least let me hold on to that. If she doesn't take it well...I don't want to add insult to injury."

He scowled. "You don't want to have sex with me in case she makes you choose, her or me." Well, that too. Something told me that as soon as I had his hands on me, that choice would become exponentially more difficult if Sonia forced it. "She won't, Rija. We're her favorite people in the world. She already calls you her sister. She'll be happy for us."

"I hope so." My chest felt tight and loose at the same time, the prospect of revealing our secret simultaneously breathed and choked air in my throat.

He studied my face. "Alright," he finally conceded. "We'll wait. House rules. But we're telling her tomorrow. Like, waking her ass up with coffee at six a.m. I want my hands on you by six fifteen."

"That's a good plan."

"I know."

We grinned at each other, hands still clasped over the coffee table. As much as it froze me in place, he was right. We'd kept this up for too long. I was ready to end it, ready to stop feeling like a horrible friend and start something better. Together. With Mal *and* with Sonia. The three of us, no more secrets.

Mal's eyes roamed down my cheek, neck, body. He swept back up all over again to rake his eyes over the top of my bustier. "So, house rules, huh?"

"How about one last ride? For old times' sake."

His smile turned downright devilish. "I was hoping you'd say that. Yours or mine?"

Sonia and I had been doing well enough in the last few years that we'd moved into a bigger, nicer place. We'd loosely labeled our third bedroom as a guest room slash pilates studio. But I didn't want him in the cold, sparsely furnished room. Not tonight.

"Mine."

Chapter 4

"Interesting," Malachi murmured, closing and locking the door behind him. "Is it cleaner than usual in here? Is that even possible?"

I'd gotten a lot done while he'd been in the other room setting up Sigmund's crate. I was practically huffing from sprinting around my room, but everything was just how I wanted it. I'd put my heels back on and perched on the edge of my sturdy oak desk. The one I'd just swept clean, dumping my computer and pen cup into my closet. I toyed with the black box he'd sent me.

"Maybe. Do you want to look from a different angle?" I nodded to the same purple chair I'd stuffed the vibrator behind earlier today. That, too, had moved. His eyes didn't leave mine as he crossed the room. I'd settled myself directly in his path, so he had to squeeze by me to sit.

He leaned back, looking like he owned the chair, the room, the whole fucking building. The top buttons of his shirt were undone, cuffs open. His legs spread and he propped himself up on his arm, thumbing his lower lip while he studied me. So cocky. And hungry. For me.

"What's your vision tonight, Kitten? You've obviously got something in mind."

"I thought, for our grand finale, a little performance."

"It's always a performance, Rija. If I'd known you were planning something special, I'd have brought a roll of ones."

"I accept Cash App." His grin flashed in the dark, the only light coming from the dim lamp in the corner. While he laughed, I leaned forward, using the arms of the chair as leverage to back myself further onto the desk.

His smile vanished. My hand brushed his, the contact jarring. I hissed.

It had occurred to me before that the nature of our interactions made us as sensitized as horny teenagers. I'd never in my life nearly come at the brush of someone's pinky against my palm. But with Malachi, and our self-imposed celibacy, all things were possible. It was all at once ridiculous and also *hot*.

"Is it still going to be this good? When we're able to touch?"

"Rija, I swear to you, and I cannot stress this enough, it will be better than anything in the history of the universe, when I'm finally able to touch you."

"The whole universe? Well, fuck, no pressure or anything." I swung my legs around until I was kneeling on the table in front of him.

His fingers swiped across his mouth. Eyes drank me in. "Oh, that's...that's just lovely." His face was level with my hips. He'd have an incredible view of the action once I got started.

"I thought you might like that." I dragged a palm up my thigh, inching my skirt up a few inches. My other hand ran the corner of the box back and forth over my collarbone. He grunted at the sight.

"What will you do first, Mal? When you can touch me tomorrow? Let me guess..." I tapped a finger to my lips, pouting while I watched him. He looked so relaxed in his body, so rigid in his face. On pins and needles. "Straight for my tits. I know how fond you are of them."

"*Errrrr*. Wrong. You've lost your unboxing privileges." He snatched the box out of my hand without having to leave his seat. We were very close. Perhaps the closest we'd ever been for such a prolonged period.

I watched his long fingers pop the tab open and slide the sleek toy out. The scent of soap and plastic rose between us. He always shipped the vibrators completely cleaned and fully stocked with fresh batteries. I'd never once received one I'd had to prep, myself.

It was the kind of proactive planning I could get behind, and just one more thing I loved about him. Sure, he was sending me a sex toy so he could watch me get off for him, but he was *thinking about me* at the same time. It was hot on many levels.

I tore my eyes away from his to look at the toy he held between us. "Oh!" I gasped.

"Thought you might like that." He copied my words from earlier, showing off how it curved at the end. The perfect angle to hit the ever-elusive g-spot. My favorite. "It has ten speeds, too. A few different modes."

"You spoil me."

"Absolutely." He twisted the base. A familiar buzzing sound filled the air. "It's your mouth, by the way. That's the first thing I want to know. How you taste. How soft that pouty lip will feel against mine. What'll it be, Kitten? Soft? Or fast?"

He touched the tip of the vibrator to my thigh. I tensed at the buzzing tickle on my skin. He rolled it up and down. The feel of it against sensitive skin reminded me too much of how it would feel slightly higher.

The thought of him holding it *there* and looking at me like he was now, like he wanted to devour me, short-circuited something in my brain. We'd never taken it that far before, with him controlling the toy. Another unspoken rule—he stayed in his corner, I stayed in mine.

Tonight, though, so close to the end of our no touching arrangement, maybe we could bend the rules. Just a little.

"Faster," I whispered. His gaze held mine as he twisted the base again. The tickling on my leg increased.

"Like that?" He growled, staring up at me, eyes dark and hooded.

"Mmm hmm." I bit my lip, teasing him. "I like it. Do you want to see how much?" I didn't wait for his permission. I inched my skirt up higher. The fabric slid up my legs, bunching at my hips to give him the perfect view of my lace-covered center. Had I sprinted into my bedroom to change underwear the second I'd had an opportunity? Yes. But the look on his face was well worth it.

He had his presents, I had mine. I'd been saving this sheer black thong, snakes twining inward from my hip bones, for a special occasion.

A groan escaped his lips. The toy halted its rolling on my thigh for a second before Mal resumed the motion.

I knew the picture I presented, and I knew how much it lit him up. He was a man of nuance, reveling in the give and take of sex, the mystery and the reveal. Having me fully clothed, shoes on, while he watched my bare pussy work a vibrator, would send him to his knees.

"Fuck, I want to come in there. Tug on it, Kitten. Work your clit for me."

I hooked my thumbs into the delicate lace straps, pulling slightly to increase the pressure of the string between my lower lips. My hips rocked nearly without a thought, sliding the lace infinitesimally up and down my clitoris.

"I'm already wet."

"Of course you are. I can see it shining on that bare pussy. How would you taste there? How would you take my tongue if I slid it up to taste you?"

Since he couldn't use his hands, his words usually ended up doing most of the work. Thankfully, Malachi was a master of the dirty talk. He could practically bring me to the edge with a pointed look and a few filthy, well-placed words. I'd need a little more than that tonight, though.

He knew it, too. "Show me what you want, Kitten." He flipped the vibrator around, offering me the base. Instead, I reached for where he held the toy, fingers sliding against his. The hairs on my arms stood on end. His skin was warm and rough.

I dragged the moment out, slipping the pads of my fingers over his knuckles one by one before plucking the toy from him. He stroked his dick over his pants, eyes looking hot.

"Careful, Ri."

"What are you going to do?" I arched a brow, sliding the humming plastic between my thighs where I craved it. I circled it around the lace between my legs, hooking my finger in the thong to move it to the side.

"Maybe nothing, tonight."

We both groaned when I slid the toy inside easily. I twisted my wrist so the crooked tip hit that perfect spot at the front.

"Maybe I'll wait until tomorrow. When I get my hands on you." His growl slid like silk around me, the words twisting my insides with anticipation. *When I get my hands on you.* A reminder that we were mere hours away from dropping all the secrets and the pretense. To just *be* together.

I gasped, working it faster.

"You like the sound of that. But think how much better you'll feel when it's my fingers stroking your pretty clit. Me inside you, not a piece of plastic. Look at me, Rija."

My eyes had drifted closed, imagining the scenario he described. My lashes flickered open at his command.

He looked like a god, sprawled against velvet, propped up on one elbow while he watched me pleasure myself. He stroked lazily at his cock, straining behind the still-closed zipper. Eyes black. Depthless.

"Tell me how I'll feel, kitten."

Oh, God. We'd done this so many times, he knew exactly what buttons to push to make me lose it. Forcing me to vocalize my thoughts, fantasies, was the greatest trick up his sleeve. He wasn't pulling punches tonight.

"Big," I sucked in a breath. "I'll be so full..."

"Mm hmm. Where will you want my mouth, Rija? You want my tongue on you? Or teeth?"

I worked my hand faster, but the toy between my legs couldn't keep up with the desire flooding me. "Both," I whispered, imagining his lips on my neck. Teeth at my collarbone.

"Greedy." He sounded like he approved.

"Only for you."

"That's right." His voice was closer. His breath teased across my cheekbones. I'd closed my eyes again. When I blinked them open, he was standing in front of me, inches away. "Just like I'm dying for you. It's only you, Rija. No one else."

We'd admitted months ago that neither of us had been seeing anyone else for a while. Say what you would about our fucked-up relationship, at least we were exclusive. Still, the reminder of that fact made me bite my lip. Twist the toy faster.

"Do you know what I would do? If I could touch you right now?"

"Mmph..." I swallowed a moan. He was so close to *actually* touching me, I could hardly think about anything else. My core tightened at having him so near. His smell—salt and limes—made me want to bury my face in his neck.

"Fuck you faster. Harder." He took a deep breath, like he was breathing me in, too. "You need more to get there, don't you?"

The image seared across my brain. *His* hand on the toy. *His* actions bringing me pleasure. After so many times doing this myself, the concept felt decadent. Necessary. And so close, I could almost taste it.

"Show me," I whispered, freezing him in place.

"You want me to take care of you tonight, Kitten?"

I shuddered, loving his choice of words. Taking care of me, because he would. He'd stop at nothing to wring every drop of pleasure from my body. My hand slowed as I nodded my head. *Yes. Yes, please.*

"You're sure about this? It's not house rules."

It was a step we'd never taken before, but so close to the end of this torturous arrangement, I couldn't help myself. I needed to know how he'd move inside me, even if it was just by proxy for tonight. "I'm sure. We're telling her tomorrow, Malachi. I need more." I could barely get the words out, already panting in anticipation of *him* giving me pleasure. *His* movements making me come.

His hand swept lower, grazing where I worked the vibrator in and out. Every muscle in my body clenched. Fingers brushed again. This time, he cupped his hand around mine, moving it in a harder rhythm.

"Fuck, Rija," he whispered, mouth so close to mine, I could swear our lips brushed. He stared down my body, taking in my breasts in the low cut top. The movement of our hands together. *Together,* taking me higher.

"Other hand, Kitten. Pet that clit for me. Keep this up. That's it."

I whimpered when he stepped back, nearly pitching off the desk as I leaned after him. It had been too good, and I hadn't had enough. I needed more, I needed all of it...

He stopped me with a warning look. The wildness in his eyes told me he was too close to snapping. "I'm playing by your rules, Ri. You wanted to put on one last show."

He unbuttoned his pants, working the zipper down. His cock sprang free, thick and hard, making my mouth water. The sight of it made my muscles clasp the toy tighter. The new pressure, combined with the quick beat Malachi had started, made me cry out softly.

He fisted his length, already jerking it hard. No soft buildup or coy strokes.

"Mal," I gasped, keeping the vibrator right...there... I was close. He was, too. I could see it in the straining of his neck. "You're...already..." I whined, head tilting back on my neck. Body bowing with pleasure.

"I've been thinking about you all day." Malachi swore, the desperation in his voice drawing my attention back. The vibrator moved at the same speed as his fist sliding up and down. I could almost imagine it was *him* inside me, hitting my g spot and making my vision sparkle. "Harder on your clit, Ri."

My fingers strummed faster, the feeling shooting my hips up an inch. Everything in me tightened, bearing down on the toy bringing me so much pleasure.

My climax washed over me, pebbling my skin. I gasped at the feeling. Sobbed that it wasn't what I wanted. Needed.

"You'll have me soon, Kitten, I promise. I'll give you everything you need. *Damn*." My lashes fluttered open. I wanted to see him when he came, too. His hand pounded his dick, hard and fast. "I would die to have that sweet pussy wrapped around me right now, instead of my fingers. You'd be so hot, Kitten. Would you suck me up? Milk me dry with how much you wanted me?"

His words were setting off more fireworks between my legs, prolonging the orgasm I didn't want to end. I couldn't bear the thought of him leaving this room.

"Yes, I want you to come inside me."

"Fuck, *fuck*, Rija." The image sent him over the edge. Thick white ropes spilled over his hand while he stroked himself. He didn't take his eyes off me.

"I want to kiss you."

I let the toy fall out of me. Clicked it off. We stared at each other. His words were bitter. Harsh and sour when we should have been sated and relaxed. I hated it, but I understood it. Regardless of how good I had just felt, I wanted *him*. Not a vibrator. The aching, jealous feeling had been getting worse and worse lately.

"Tomorrow, Mal," I whispered, setting the toy aside and sitting down to let my legs swing off the edge of the desk. I swallowed under the weight of his gaze.

"I'd loop that hair around my fist. Mouth on yours. Suck on your tongue." His hand ran down his face. Eyes finally left mine, squeezing shut. "Clean you up. Hold you. Sleep with you in my arms."

"Tomorrow, Cariño."

He grimaced, his head hitting the back of the chair. His eyes raked over me as he wiped his other hand on his pants. He loved when I called him that. *My sweetheart.* The same thing my grandmother had called my grandfather before he passed.

"I hate this." He stood, brushing against my legs.

"I'm sorry," I whispered down at my lap. It was always like this now. One amazing thrill and then...the emptiness. I wanted him to kiss me. Hold me. As much as I loved him, I hated this, too.

"It's not your fault, Kitten. Just a few more hours and then..." His hand hovered over my cheek. I wanted to feel it on my skin.

"Just a few more."

He left, casting one last look backwards as he tucked himself back into his pants. I brushed my teeth and peeled out of my birthday outfit, opting for an extra-large T-shirt that said, *"educated drug dealer"* on the front and *"nurse practitioner"* on the back. My sheets were cold. My pillow wouldn't bunch up the way I wanted it to. I couldn't get rid of the prickly feeling in my chest.

It was ridiculous, I knew. We'd tell Sonia tomorrow. And then we'd be together. It was silly to be sad tonight. But I was.

My door opened softly.

"I thought, if I can't be close to you tonight, maybe he could?"

Mal tipped a sleepy Sigmund onto my bed. The puppy pawed around for a moment before curling up in the crook of my shoulder, his little nose resting on my neck.

My eyes prickled, but this time, it had nothing to do with sadness.

I love you. I almost whispered. But not right now. Not before we'd ever even kissed. Tomorrow, maybe.

"Thank you," I said instead.

He twined his fingers with mine, pressing a kiss to the back of my hand. Definitely against the rules. Definitely what I needed right at this moment. How did he always know?

I slept soundly with my dog all night, waiting for tomorrow.

Chapter 5

"Birthday cheers!" Sonia clinked her non-alcoholic sangria against mine. We usually needed a detox after a blowout like last night. "I'm sorry I was MIA today, but things were *happening* from like start to finish. Very glad I get to slow down and have some more bday fun with you. I'm even putting my phone away, but remind me to tell you later about the insane text I got from my old college roommate." She made a show of slipping her phone into her purse, gesturing at it like she was Vanna White, talking a mile a minute the whole time. Sonnie was a little manic sometimes, but I loved her.

"It's not my birthday anymore," I reminded her, taking a sip and lowering my sunglasses over my eyes. I'd fared better than she did, but with another birthday came another reminder that I wasn't in my mid-twenties anymore. Things like hangovers and muscle aches had a tendency to sneak up on me these days.

"Birthday is a state of mind, Ri. If you're not celebrating for, like, a week, what are you even doing?"

"Fair." I took a sip, glancing around the patio of my favorite tapas place. Malachi was due any minute now, and I was practically levitating in my seat with impatience.

We'd planned to tell Rija together, but a work emergency had pulled him out of the apartment early this morning, before I'd even woken up. He'd been gone all day, dealing with problems at the Chicago office he'd sneakily started setting up weeks ago.

Sonia had also been in and out since the morning, running errands, getting a mani/pedi, and grabbing lunch with one of her travel nurse friends. I'd been wound up since my alarm had gone off, waiting to get them to sit still in the same place so I could confess and get all this out in the open. Now, on the patio with a pitcher of glorified juice on the table, it was finally about to happen.

If he would just get here, already.

"Seriously, Ri. You deserve to celebrate. Like, a lot. I couldn't ask for a better friend. The way you've stuck by me through everything with that horrible breakup last year and my job drama... I love you, girl. You know that, right?" Sonia's green eyes were wide, earnest. My heart squeezed with affection and guilt.

Sonnie had been with me through the worst life offered, too, like my parents cutting me off and my grandmother's Alzheimer's diagnosis. I could only hope she'd keep sticking by me when everything was out in the open tonight.

"You're my best friend, Sonnie. I love you, too."

"I know, but I wanted to say thank you."

Oh, God, please don't thank me when I'm about to tell you I've been lying to you for months. "You don't have to do that."

She studied me, brows drawn, serious in a way she usually wasn't. "I do. You've been so great about Malachi. I have a few issues there, you know? And I've never once had to worry about you ditching me for him."

"O-oh…" For perhaps the first time in my life, I was at a loss for words. She reached over to rub her hand over my forearm.

"I know this seems like it's coming out of nowhere, but I was thinking about it last night, watching you together and knowing you have my back, no matter what. I love how close you two have gotten."

The only response I had for her was a tight grin. I moved my arm away to wipe my palms on the skirt of my dress. I was the worst person in the world.

"You should know—Oh, Siggy!" she sang, standing to greet the dog who shot to our table, the new leather leash I'd gotten him this morning trailing on the sidewalk. The other patrons grinned and cooed at him. God, he was so cute.

I'd spent all morning with the puppy and felt like he already owned half of my heart. At least, the pieces that weren't already bought and paid for by the Dobrev siblings.

He was sweet and squirmy and though I'd hated to leave him in the crate for dinner, I wasn't sure inviting a puppy to such a serious conversation was a good idea. Malachi, looking harried and striding down the sidewalk with his phone glued to his face, apparently thought differently.

He loitered at the edge of the patio, watching Sigmund try to jump into my lap. Mal's face was thunderous. I couldn't make out his words, but he paced, hand on his hip and shaking his head at intervals.

"Yikes. Wonder what that's about." Sonia gave the puppy another scratch on the chin before she ducked inside the restaurant to ask for a bowl of water.

"Christ," Mal hissed, tossing his phone on the table and bracing his hands against the metal top. He stared while Siggy licked my face. "I will give you a million dollars if you let me kiss you right now."

My stomach clenched. I really wanted to. "Bad day?"

He collapsed into a chair, the metal legs scraping against the concrete. "The worst. I'm sorry. I know we were supposed to talk to Sonnie earlier." He reached out like he wanted to run his fingers over my shoulder, but pulled back, his hand fisting.

"I figured we'd leave this guy at home?" I rocked Siggy in my arms, where he was content to snuggle.

Mal's palms scraped down his face. "That's the fucking thing. He had to come with me. I'm leaving straight from here to go to the airport."

"What?" I sucked in a breath, blew it out. Malachi was a Big Deal. I knew that. The people around us had already started nudging each other and looking over at our table. But most of the time, when it was just us, or hanging out at a party like last night, I only saw him as mine. My Malachi.

It was easy to forget, when we were laughing like morons over a Rick and Morty episode, that he was a serious entrepreneur worth millions and millions of dollars. When work stuff did pop up, I tried to be understanding. I worked in an intense job, too. Things happened.

But tonight...I'd thought this discussion with Sonia was a priority for him. I'd thought us clearing the air and then actually *being together* was a big deal. I knew, logically, that a relationship with me was small fries compared with his multi-million dollar enterprise, but I couldn't help but feel disappointed.

"I know, Kitten, I, *fuck*, I'm sorry." He reached out again, this time closing his fingers around mine. "You are important to me. More important than work. I wouldn't be here right now if that wasn't true. There's just...a fire I can't put out long-distance."

My heart fluttered at the feel of his hand on mine. "I understand." I glanced down at where Siggy had settled into my lap.

Mal's grip tightened. "Look at me, Rija. It's important to me that you know you're my priority. Always. If I had any other option, I'd park my ass on your couch for the next month."

I met his eyes. He looked concerned. Underneath that, a little crazed, which wasn't his usual style. "I believe you. Mal, what happened—"

"Whoa, you two look serious. Need me to leave?" Sonia set the bowl down by my feet and plopped into her chair.

Mal sat back as well, releasing my hand. My fingers felt cold, even when I buried them in Siggy's fur. He sighed. "*I* have to leave, Sonnie."

Her head whipped around from where she'd been air kissing the dog's nose. "Leave? I thought you were here for a while?"

"Yeah, that was the original plan." He raked fingers through his hair. It looked like he'd done that multiple times today. "Very crappy thing back in Colorado. Somehow coinciding with contracting issues in Chicago. Real shit storm."

"But you'll be back in town for the gala next week, right?" Sonia pressed, her brow furrowed. She leaned into the table like his answer was critical.

"The gala where I'm the keynote speaker? Yes, I'll be back for that," he drawled. "That's move-in day, anyway."

Sonia relaxed back into her chair. "I can't believe you set all this up behind our backs. Sneaky brother."

"I like a good surprise." He stole a sip from my sangria, grimacing when he realized it didn't have any wine in it.

Sonia snorted. "Yeah, but you can't keep a secret for shit."

His eyes flashed to mine. Was it time? Did this feel like too soon? Too rushed? When did he need to leave? He nodded, giving me the encouragement I needed, steeling me. Siggy grumbled and jumped down as I sat forward. "Listen, Sonnie. There's something—"

"I can't keep a secret either, though! I'm going to New York tomorrow." A smug smile tilted her lips.

"—we have... New York?" My carefully thought-out confession died on my lips.

Sonia bounced in her seat. "Yes! I just took a last-minute contract over there. My friend Shaina is going for a few months and said they needed another nurse, so, Big Apple, here I come!"

"Tomorrow?" Mal sounded as shocked as I felt.

Sonia was a travel nurse, which meant she took jobs and contracts with hospitals all over the city. Demand for nurses was high, and it meant she could jump around from place to place without being tied down. She enjoyed the freedom it gave her, not to mention the sizable paychecks.

But Sonia hadn't taken a gig outside of Chicago in years. Not since her first few months out of nursing school.

"I'm a free spirit, Ri, but that doesn't mean I enjoy sleeping in temporary housing," she'd informed me, shuddering.

"I didn't know you were looking for a job outside of the city." She was between contracts right now, and I knew she'd been shopping around for her next gig for a few weeks. She could afford to be picky, and this seemed...sudden.

Sonia topped off her glass from the pitcher, shaking her head like I was the crazy one. "No, silly. Nothing like that. I know it's last minute, but Shaina and I just happened to hook up today for lunch and she mentioned it. It's only a few weeks. Eight, tops. It'll be good to get out. Shake things up a little."

"Two months? I'm moving in next week." The tic in Malachi's jaw told me this was one more piece of unexpected news on top of an already overwhelming day. I wanted to stroke his leg, still the bouncing he'd started without realizing it.

"You'll have some time to acclimate to the city while I'm not here. It'll be good for you." She beamed at us. "Rija will be here to show you around!"

Heat flooded my face, body flashing hot when I thought about spending weeks and weeks with Malachi without having to tiptoe around Sonia. It would be...incredible. So freeing and nice and we could sleep in the same bed and...

I felt instantly ashamed at how excited I got at the thought. I heaved a sigh. This had to end. Now.

"Sonia, Malachi and I—"

"You'll be fine! But you'll have to be his date to the gala, since I won't be around. He needs protection from all the thirsty housewives."

Unbidden, my attention snagged on Mal. He was scowling, but the only thing I could picture in my brain was him in a tux. He went to a lot of fancy events, so he had several, and looked smoking hot in every one of them. He glanced at me, eyes doing a double-take when he caught me staring.

"Sonia..." He started, without taking his eyes off me.

"It might be weird, but you two might want to get a little touchy-feely for that one."

My thoughts screeched to a halt. Mal's head snapped towards his sister. Had she just...

"What?"

"Those housewives can get feral at the auction. Probably best if you guys act like you're together, you know? Maybe they'll leave you alone when they realize they can't compete with your hot Latina girlfriend." Her straw rattled as she slurped up the remains of her sangria. "I'm glad I got to tell you both in person, but I gotta hop if I want to finish packing tonight. My flight's at the ass crack of dawn tomorrow." She rolled her eyes.

"Sonia, wait! I need to talk—"

"I didn't mean to spring this on you. It'll be okay, Ri." She squeezed my shoulder a few times, inching out from the table.

"You'll have Malachi while I'm gone. And when I come back in a few weeks, we'll all settle back in."

She barely paused to pet Siggy's head before bustling onto the sidewalk.

I stared after her, mouth ajar. Siggy whined to see her leave.

"You want me to go chase her down?" Mal refilled Sonia's glass before taking a sip.

"How are you so calm right now? She wouldn't let us get a word in. This was supposed to happen today!" My napkin twisted in my hands.

Mal shrugged. "She gave us an official moratorium on the no touching rule. That solves the vast majority of my current problems."

"Your current problems include contract disputes and emergencies back in Colorado."

"Like I said, biggest of my problems. Solved. Come here." He lunged, hauling my chair closer and dragging his palm up my calf. He groaned. In public. Audibly. I barely suppressed the full-body shudder his hands instigated.

"Mal," I gasped. "We have to tell her." I leaned closer. I wanted more of his hands on me. Higher.

"We will." He leaned in, too. We were inches away from each other. "But maybe this is a good thing. What were we going to tell her today? That we've been having air sex for the last six months?"

"I wouldn't call it air sex…" I grumbled, shifting my knee to feel the slide of my skin against his. I wanted him to move his hand, but he kept it still, aside from a slow circling of his fingertips against my calf.

"Now, though, think about it. She gets back from New York. We tell her we got closer, physically, at the gala. That there's been something going on for a while, but we didn't act on it until then. She's practically giving us an opening, Ri."

"You're a therapist. Aren't you supposed to be against lying?"

"What part of that is a lie?"

Hmm. He had a point. Telling her about our relationship like that would soften the blow. Maybe we could even soft-launch it while she was in New York. Send her some pictures of us together. Let her get used to the idea instead of just dumping it all on her at once: *I'm in love with your brother and he makes me come with nothing but his eyes and we've been air fucking in secret for months behind your back.*

"Air fucking." I murmured, staring at his lips. They curved into a smile.

"You're right, that is better."

"So...what now?"

Finally, *finally*, his fingers inched up past my knee, splaying on my thigh. I gasped.

"Now, we—"

His phone buzzed on the table between us. I looked at it before he did. He couldn't seem to drag his eyes off my face. I blanched at the notification on the screen.

"Your flight leaves in forty-five minutes? Mal, you're not going to make it." We were miles away from the airport and he was sitting here like he had all the time in the world to rev my engine with some hungry looks and a few strokes of my leg.

"I'll make it. Give me ten minutes in a bathroom stall and I'll still make it." His hand rose higher, thumb brushing the hem of my skirt.

"Mal," I gasped, arching in my chair. We were in public, for fuck's sake, but I couldn't control my body's reaction to him.

"Five. No, three. I can make it good for you in three, Kitten." He purred. The heat he stirred up wound through my veins as his phone sounded once more.

I looked again. Two messages from his publicist slash executive assistant, Adam.

I know you're not on your way to the airport.

If you don't leave now, the Malvern situation is only going to get worse.

"What's the Malvern situation?" I asked, forcing myself to focus on the task at hand. As much as I would love three minutes in a bathroom stall with him, he had a flight to catch.

Mal jerked like I'd tossed the pitcher of icy sangria over his head. His hand fell from my leg. "Fuck. Sorry. Fuck, I have to go."

His face looked wary. He leaned over to cup my cheek in his palm. "I promise you, if it were any other issue than this one specific thing, I would already have you up against the bathroom wall right now. Do you believe me?"

"Y-yes."

His thumb brushed my bottom lip. "I want to kiss you."

"You can now." The thought made my heart leap in my chest. What would it feel like? To have his lips on mine? To grab him whenever I wanted?

He swallowed, focused on my lips. I leaned forward an inch. He was so close to me. Just a little further...

"Not here. If I kiss you now, I'm never getting on that plane. And I want you all to myself the first time."

He leaned in anyway, turning at the last second to brush a kiss across my cheek. My jaw. His teeth nipped. I sighed, breath uneven.

He cursed, then he was gone, standing and wrapping Siggy's leash around his wrist.

"I'll call you when I land. I'm so sorry, Kitten..." His teeth clicked when he bit them together. After one last look at me, he turned. The puppy trilled and whined while Mal stomped away down the sidewalk.

Chapter 6

"Miss—"

"No, really, it's fine!" I waved a jittery hand at my driver and slid out of the matte black Range Rover. The door slammed shut, blocking out the slick, low-lit interior and the smell of new leather.

"I'd have stayed in the car," Sonia chimed unhelpfully in my ear.

"Of course you would have stayed in the car. The driver was hot," I muttered, navigating the sidewalk leading to the Lincoln Zoo. Most times, I'd have stayed in the car, too. Mal had gone all out with whatever car service he'd hired to pick me up.

The new model SUV was pristine. The driver had been polite and obviously very experienced navigating Chicago traffic, getting me across town to the zoo in no time. He'd even worn an earpiece. I wasn't sure what sort of emergency driver situations would warrant an earpiece, or know who would be on the other side of the line, but it was official as hell. While I appreciated the obviously high caliber of the services being rendered, I'd been too antsy all day—all week, really—to sit still for any longer.

My gold heels clicked on the concrete as I strode past the long line of Beemers and Escalades jockeying to drop guests off at the entrance. Around me, other gala attendants stood out with their tuxes and silk gowns, lining up to get into the event venue. Apparently, this year's gala benefitting the Children's Hospital was going to be lit.

"Wait, you didn't say he was hot. Why didn't you tell me he was hot? How hot?"

"Umm," I tried to remember the guy's face. I had registered that he'd been attractive, with lots of muscles underneath that black button down, but truth be told, I hadn't been able to focus on anything but the thought of seeing Malachi.

I hadn't been able to switch shifts, so I'd been stuck in the OR all day. I'd emerged, feet sore and body sweaty, to a barrage of texts from him. One when his plane touched down in Chicago. Later, a photo of his brand new apartment key in his hand. Then, a photo of a king-sized bed, perfectly made up, surrounded by cardboard boxes. He had not bothered to add a caption to the picture. I'd still gotten the point.

Now, not only was he here, in my city, but he was here, like, just a few yards away. I shuffled up to a line snaking around the sidewalk, joining the other gala guests waiting to get inside.

"God, you're the worst! No wonder you're in a dry spell. You can't even properly describe a hot guy. I need hair color, height, distinguishing markings." Sonia's voice pulled me back onto the sidewalk and out of my head, where I was fixated on Malachi's bed, made up just for me.

Her call couldn't have come at a better time. After a week alone in our apartment, I felt like I was going crazy. Though, that could have been because Malachi had also been ridiculously busy ever since he'd left me on the patio with a half-full pitcher of virgin sangria.

I couldn't really blame him. It was a tall order to hand off responsibilities at the clinic he'd founded in Colorado five years ago. Despite having secretly worked on this move to Chicago for months, I got the feeling he was having a harder time letting go than he'd admit. His social media channels might have made him famous, but his clinical work was his true passion.

On the rare occasions I'd been able to reach him for a FaceTime call this week, he'd looked harried, maybe even a little sad. He did his best to hide it, and he'd almost succeeded once he started describing in full sensory detail what he'd do to me when he saw me next, when he could *actually touch me. Oh, my God!*

But after we hung up, usually a little breathless and grinning like fools, I couldn't quite forget the shadow of worry in his eyes.

I stepped forward as the line moved up. I'd just have to assess him in person. When I saw him. In mere minutes. And all the barriers of secrets and rules and guilt would be gone, just like that. *Poof*. I clenched shaking fingers around my gold clutch, mouth dry as a desert.

"He was tall. Dark hair," I offered. I had at least noticed that when he'd opened the car door for me back at the apartment. "Muscle-y."

She groaned as I moved up a few more paces until I could see the entrance. "The hot driver is completely squandered on you. I should be there, reaping the rewards of his attractiveness. Did he hit on you? I bet he hit on you. You look hot."

"You sure? I feel like a mess." I glanced down at my red dress, wishing for the thousandth time today I'd had more time to get ready. As it was, I'd practically sprinted into my apartment for a quick shower, thrown my dress on, and barely had time to dab on some makeup and sloppily curl a few chunks of my hair.

"Yes, I'm sure! Stop being a bitch and tell yourself how beautiful you are. Why are you being so rude to my best friend? Say it. Out loud, right now. Go on."

It felt good to laugh. It released some of the tension that built with every step I took towards the entrance. I was close, just a few people ahead of me. "I'm beautiful," I repeated obediently, wrinkling my nose at the woman in front of me, who'd looked back at my declaration.

"You are," she agreed. "Love that dress." We shared a smile before she turned back to her date. I loved people sometimes.

"See? That lady knew." Sonia crunched on something on her end of the line. "Who was she?"

"Another attendee here. We're all in line to get in. I'm not sure what the hold up...oh, dang." The crowd parted, and I got a look at what was taking so long. A team of black-clad security officers were patiently combing through purses and patting down dinner jackets. "There's security here. Like a lot. Who knew the children's hospital fundraiser would be so ritzy?"

"Weird. There wasn't security last year. Are the security people hot? Let's try to be more detailed this time, Ri."

"I, um," I smiled at the security officer who gestured me forward. "Just a sec."

I offered him my clutch right as Sonia screeched in my ear. "Not just a sec! Is. The. Security. Dude. Hot? Report. I need a description. I want to feel like I'm right there, Ri."

The man in front of me grinned, obviously overhearing her loud demands. He poked a flashlight through my lipstick and my ID. "Well?" His deep voice rumbled with barely restrained laughter. "Your friend is waiting."

Sonia gasped in my ear. "Wait, he sounded hot. *SIR, PLEASE DESCRIBE YOURSELF.*" Her voice yelled out of my phone, making me laugh even while I pulled it away from my ear. Leave it to my best friend to have some sort of long-distance flirtation with a man she'd never met. I loved her so much, even if my cheeks were burning.

"Six-two. Brown hair, green eyes. Tattoos." He returned my clutch with a wicked smile. "Single."

"*SIR, MY FRIEND IS ALSO SINGLE. SHE—*"

Oh, hell no. I didn't need Sonia setting me up on a blind date all the way from New York. Especially when she was the one who didn't know what the guy looked like. Even if he was admittedly rather attractive.

"I'm not, actually," I interrupted, shaking my head at the man. His shirt had a white embroidered logo that said *RISI Securities—Asher*. "I'm meeting someone."

"*THAT IS CORRECT, SHE IS MEETING SOMEONE. HOWEVER, I AM SINGLE.*" Sonia changed tack on a dime. I shushed her, backing away while Asher grinned.

"My friend is single and also ridiculous," I informed Asher as he waved a security wand over my dress. It clicked benignly. "She also said this thing didn't have security last year."

He shrugged, stepping back to clear the way for me. "Big hotshot celebrity here tonight. Gotta keep the crazies away."

"*SIR, IT MIGHT NOT SEEM LIKE IT, BUT I AM NOT CRAZY. JUST IN NEED OF SOME GOOD DI-*"

"Thank you, Asher. Have a nice night." I cut Sonia off, covering my whole phone with my hand to drown her out. Asher cackled.

"If your friend's as pretty as you, tell her I'd be interested."

Even though I covered the receiver, we both heard Sonia squeal. I gave Asher a mock glare. "Look what you've done." I wiggled my phone at him. It sounded like some sort of pealing alarm was going off on the other side of the line. He shot another wicked, unrepentant grin my way.

"Enjoy your evening," he winked, gesturing for someone behind me to step forward.

In the several minutes it took to shush Sonia and convince her I would not turn back around and take Asher's picture, I made my way to Café Brauer, where the main event was being hosted.

"Okay, I'm here now, thank you for humiliating me in front of strangers, yet again." I had to raise my volume as I walked in, the voices and clatter of hundreds of people echoing off the polished hard woods. I handed my wrap to a smiling coat check attendant and waited for a ticket.

"Any time, babe. Remember, your objective is simple. Keep the cougars off my brother. I swear, last year, one of them tried to crawl into his lap."

"Right. I'm on it," I told her, turning back to the teeming room. What I couldn't tell her was that I, myself, planned to crawl into Malachi's lap soon, so there likely wouldn't be room for anyone else. I nabbed a glass of champagne from a passing server's tray.

"I'm serious, Ri. Stick with him. Get up in there. Protect his virtue."

"Mm hmm." I downed the drink in a few gulps. I would not be protecting Malachi Dobrev's virtue tonight. Not even a little. "Listen, I gotta go. I need to go find him."

"I love you. Be good but not too good. Let loose a little, Ri. You've been working that juicy booty off. You deserve to have some fun tonight."

A beep in my ear made me pull my phone back. Malachi's name flashed across the screen. My heart leaped. "I will, love you!" I hung up on Sonnie, switching the call to Mal.

"Hello?"

"It's six oh five. You were supposed to be in my arms five minutes ago." Mal's voice sank into me like a caress, even as the background noise on his end clashed with the chatter I heard in real time from the people around me. "Where are you?"

I glanced around, trying to orient myself. The café was a popular spot for these types of functions. High-end weddings and corporate fundraisers. The setup was a familiar one.

Candles gleamed from the tables that circled the room, leaving space for a dance floor in the center. Fun, colorful flower arrangements were dotted here and there. A jazz band crooned on a stage, just soft enough not to disturb the conversations throughout the room. They'd probably crank up the volume for dancing after dinner and the auction.

Digital screens around the room scrolled through images of what would be auctioned off tonight, as well as pictures and stories of children who would benefit from our donations.

"I'm on the left side. Near one of the screens."

"Left side from the stage? Or the door?" He sounded urgent, rushed like the pulse pounding through my veins. This was it. *This was it.* I was about to be face-to-face with Malachi Dobrev and there was nothing stopping me from grabbing him the way I wanted. Kissing him. Feeling him against me. Stripping him out of his tux later and running my hands down his chest.

My heart squeezed. "The stage. I'm circling around."

"I'm towards the middle. What are you wearing?"

Malachi had asked me that question over the phone many times in the last few months. I'd never heard him say the words with such frustrated desperation.

"Red. Silk." I scooted around a table, heading into the melee.

"I...that's not you. Wait, I...*Rija.*"

I turned, the whispered wonder in his voice steering me, somehow. And there he was, staring at me, looking like a Calvin Klein model. Jaw freshly shaved, hair combed back from his face. He had a rainbow polka dot handkerchief sticking artfully out of his pocket. The perfect counterbalance of whimsy to what would otherwise be a devastating package.

"Mal."

Despite the people milling back and forth in front of us, he smiled like he heard me. I realized we were still holding our phones to our ears, standing in the middle of a fancy party, gazing at each other like star-crossed lovers from across the room.

He slid his phone in to his breast pocket while he strode toward me. I stumbled to meet him halfway, shoving my phone back into my purse to free my hands up for...for what, I wasn't sure. This moment had played a starring role in my fantasies—both PG and X rated—all week long.

Would he sweep me into a chaste kiss? Would I leap into his arms? Would we haul each other into the coat closet? (Those specific daydreams got X rated, fast.)

He strode forward, turning to slip past a woman in a sparkly navy dress, and then he was *there,* arms reaching around me, pulling me into his chest.

"Rija." He sounded like he'd been searching for me his whole life. Like he'd been waiting for too long to have me here—right here, in this room, in this dress, in his arms.

I understood the feeling. I buried my face against his neck as his hand ran up my spine to bury into my hair. He breathed me in. My arms clasped around him, feeling the muscles of his back flex through his jacket as we swayed in place.

In the middle of a crowded ballroom, surrounded by strangers, it felt like coming home. So momentous my throat tightened.

His chest shuddered against mine as he breathed once more, inhaling deeply. His fingers flexed, massaging my scalp before slipping downwards to cup the back of my neck, stroking over the sensitive spot behind my ear. I shivered.

"Hi, Mal."

I grinned into his skin. There was a strong likelihood that my lipstick would smudge all over his collar and I didn't give a fuck. Actually, the thought made me ridiculously happy. I nuzzled him once more, feeling territorial.

"Hi, Kitten. Christ, you smell...so good."

I laughed, clenching him tighter to me. "I worked a ten today and barely had time to shave my legs. I smell like a hospital." An unfortunate fact: when you worked ten hours straight in the OR, you ended up smelling like latex gloves and alcohol wipes.

"Not true. You smell like flowers and Rija. My favorite." His hand traveled down my neck, stroking over the skin between my shoulder blades. He grunted. I nearly purred.

"Rija," he began. He had that tortured, if-you-don't-move-the-vibrator-and-get-yourself-off-*right-now,* I'm-going-to-jump-through-the-screen-to-get-my-hands-on-you tone I'd heard from him many times before. Well, he had his hands on me, now.

I couldn't wait to hear what he was finally going to do about it.

Chapter 7

"Malachi!" A man's booming voice sounded from somewhere behind Mal. I glanced around to find its source. Instead, I saw a woman eyeing us from a huddle of people to my right. I guess I'd have to wait to find out what he was going to do now that his hands were all over me.

"I think we're causing a scene," I whispered, inching away just far enough to look up at his beautiful face. His dark eyes were nearly black. Sharp and hungry.

"I'm about to cause a scene, if someone tries to pull me away from you," he muttered, his gaze skimming down my face to my chest where the silk fell in a daring vee.

"There you are, my man!" The voice came closer.

Mal's eyes lingered on my skin. "Too late to ditch this place?"

"Aren't you the keynote?" I murmured, even though I'd love nothing more than to drag him away to somewhere private and yank the tux right off his body.

"Ah, no wonder you took off in such a hurry."

Mal sighed, his breath stirring a few curls laying across my shoulder. With one last, lingering stroke down my back, he stepped away, hauling me close to his side while we both faced the vaguely familiar middle-aged man who'd approached us.

"Frank, allow me to introduce my girlfriend, Marija Sanchez. She's a nurse over at Ced...ar..." His words ended in an awkward cough. In the process of introducing me, Mal had finally gotten an eyeful of the rest of my dress.

It was little flashy without being totally slutty (not that I minded slutty, depending on the day). Thin straps held up the deep panels of the bodice, cinching at my waist before giving way to a fall of red silk and a slit that was, admittedly, a little on the sluttier side of flashy.

I barely had the wherewithal to enjoy the look on his face. My brain was still replaying him calling me his girlfriend. A shiver worked its way through me. Mal's fingers clenched tighter on my waist.

"Well, of course I know Marija. Carl's girl!" The man leaned forward to offer his hand, unaware of the delicious tension he was interrupting. "You might not remember me. Franklin Pearce."

I blinked, wrenching my eyes away from Mal to the man in front of us. No wonder he looked familiar. He was the president of the medical school over at Northwestern and a prominent member of the Chicago medical scene. "Dr. Pearce. Of course I remember you. Lovely to see you again."

He pumped my hand enthusiastically, his other clutching a nearly empty tumbler of amber liquid. "Sanchez. That man's a machine. I was on the board with him at the Cancer Research Center. Did more in a week than most of us did all year. You want something done, you call Carl. Incredible man. Have you met him?" he asked Mal, finally letting go of me.

"I'm familiar with his work." Mal's fingers brushed the tie at my waist, words abrupt, gaze flat. I frowned at him. Mal was known all around the world for his warm, charismatic charm. Bring up my family, though, and he was suddenly frostier than a snowman.

"Amazing man." Frank barreled on as if he hadn't noticed the icy tone in Mal's voice.

"Yes, amazing," I repeated, glancing around. If he was going to extol my father's virtues for the foreseeable future, I'd need another glass of champagne.

"You still involved with the research center? I hear good things," Mal cut in, saving me.

Frank's face lit up. "Yes, indeed! Just had some amazing trial results cross my desk..."

I slid my hand under Mal's jacket to stroke his side, thanking him for the assist while Frank droned on. Malachi returned the favor in the form of a caress at my waist. A grabby one. Like he was clutching at me. Like he couldn't get enough.

I bit my lip to contain the quickly spreading smile on my face. The earlier prickle of unease about my family vanished like magic. Mal and Dr. Pearce chatted some more about the research center before Mal spotted someone in the crowd.

"Dierdre! Have you met Dr. Pearce?" He waved a blonde woman over to where we stood.

"Dr. Dobrev, so good to see you!" She smiled, the tight skin of her face stretching as much as the Botox would allow. "I haven't had the pleasure. Dierdre Harrington." She extended her hand to Frank, then to me. I opened my mouth to introduce myself, but Mal beat me to it.

"This is Rija Sanchez. My girlfriend."

"Harrington? The one they're naming that new wing of the children's hospital after? Must've cost a pretty penny." Frank chortled, throwing back the remains of his glass. Dierdre demurred, saying something about the importance of giving back. I tuned them out, watching Mal snatch two glasses of champagne from a passing server.

"You're throwing that girlfriend title around pretty liberally tonight," I murmured, taking a flute from him. His fingers smoothed across my hip again.

"That a problem?" His eyes twinkled as he took a sip, my stomach fizzing like the bubbles in his wine.

"No. No problem."

"Good. Because I'm planning to throw it around a lot more."

As the man of the hour, it seemed like Mal was passed from group to group for the rest of the night. He didn't miss an opportunity to introduce me as his girlfriend and found every excuse imaginable to touch me. I was just as bad, stroking the muscles of his back and leaning into his body at every opportunity.

His speech was flawless. He was poignant, witty and hopeful. And after he stepped off the stage to a standing ovation, every ounce of his attention had been focused on me. I'm sure dinner was lovely, though I could hardly remember it. Mal took full advantage of the high slit on my skirt, stroking the bare skin of my thigh under the white tablecloth, always stopping at the top, just short of getting under my skirt. Holy fuck, I wanted him under my skirt so badly.

"Hope you're ready for a bidding war, dear," Dierdre whispered as a man on the stage announced the auction was about to start.

"Bidding war?" I might have misheard her. My mind was so wholly in the gutter, my thoughts weren't working properly. Mal's fingers tightened on my thigh. Another rush of warmth flooded between my legs. We needed to get out of here soon, before we set the room on fire.

"I assume you don't want him to go on that lunch date with anyone else. Better be quick!" She patted her bidding paddle, smiling indulgently at me before turning her attention back to the stage.

"Lunch date?" I hissed to Mal. He leaned forward to wrap his arm around my shoulders, fingers circling my skin.

"Lunch..." he trailed off, eyes catching on the low neckline of my dress for a moment. "I auction off a lunch with a fan every year. And I want to lick you right there."

"Right here?" My fingers slipped up my chest, tracing the line of silk across my breast. He nodded, captivated. "Maybe that's something you can do at lunch. How much do these dates usually run a gal?"

I wasn't swimming in cash like the people around me, but I'd dip into savings if I needed to. I wanted that lunch date. And a dinner date. And a morning-after date. All Mal's dates were mine, now.

His eyes snapped to mine, shining. "Don't worry about the cost. You're going to win."

***

"Holy fuck."

My heart was racing, cheeks aflame. I fanned myself with an auction brochure. I was fairly certain that I was as close to a panic attack as I'd ever been in my 29 years of life.

"You did so well, Kitten," Malachi murmured, guiding me past tables and well-wishers. Mostly. I caught the eye of the brunette across the room, who had been gunning for the lunch date hard. She practically snarled at me.

Oh, fuck. "Oh, fuck."

Mal kneaded my shoulder, steering me to the side of the room and waving at a few folks along the way. Someone grabbed him to say something, and I stood there, swaying on my feet. I was probably in shock.

"Twenty thousand..." Sweat prickled on my neck as Mal said goodbye to whoever he was talking to and led me through the maze of tables once more. The building's AC had cranked up. The contrast of my heated, adrenaline-filled body and the frigid air pumping through the vents made me feel even more off-kilter.

I'd never spent twenty thousand dollars on anything before. I'm not sure I'd ever even spent five thousand on anything.

"And you won't have to today." Mal smiled back at me as we neared a table with a sign that said "Settlement Desk". Apparently, the shock of spending so much money with just a few raises of my arm had made me babble out loud. "I told you, I'll cover you. I'll even pay for lunch. How about that?"

"We just spent *twenty thousand dollars* to go out to lunch together, and it doesn't even include the meal?" My head was still reeling, had been since we broke into the five-figure range. The women in that room had been ruthless. It had been an absolute madhouse the second Mal's face popped up as the next item up for auction. Towards the end, Mal'd had to nudge my arm to make sure I kept bidding. "Bullshit. You're taking me to McDonalds. I'm getting a Happy Meal."

"Rija," he snorted, reaching into his breast pocket to pull out a checkbook.

"I'm serious. You'll never financially recover from this." I laughed at the sheer ridiculousness of it. He hauled me into his side, nose nuzzling my neck.

"What's a few grand for an opportunity to have you all to myself for a few hours?"

The woman seated behind the table rifled through some papers and slid them across the table for us to sign. Mal watched carefully when I penned my signature with shaking hands.

"See? Now you're contractually obligated to go on a date with me. I've locked you down, Kitten. No price could be too high." He winked as he wrote in the checkbook.

I scoffed, like his ridiculous flirting didn't affect me, when all I really wanted to do was haul him into the shrubbery and have my way with him. "Look at you, paying for dates and using a checkbook. How old are you, anyway? I'm going to start calling you Duck McScrooge."

I peered over his shoulder just as he ripped the check off the pad, handing it to the woman face-down. He wasn't fast enough. I'd seen all six figures on that check.

I gasped, eyes going wide. "Mal—"

"Rija! There you are. Quite a show you put on back there." My mother, *oh God, of all people, my MOTHER*, strode up to the table. My back straightened, posture correcting automatically in some ridiculous Pavlovian response to her voice.

My *mother* was here? My parents were supposed to be at some conference in California. At least, that was the excuse she gave me when she'd informed me they weren't available for dinner on my birthday. Not that I'd asked.

"You could have worn something less revealing tonight. Especially if you were going to make a spectacle of yourself," she muttered, brushing a perfunctory kiss on my cheek before turning to beam at Mal. She fluffed her black, shoulder-length hair. It was graying, but you'd never know it. She paid her hair dresser good money to take that secret to the grave.

Her high-necked black gown accentuated her tiny waist. Small but mighty was mom's M.O. Only a spine of steel could have kept up with my dad all these years and not let him run roughshod all over her. No, no. If my dad was the ladder-climber, mom was his spotter. Always on the lookout for the next opportunity. The next good connection. And now there was one right in front of her.

"Doctor Dobrev, Rosalia Sanchez. Such a pleasure to meet you." She thrust her hand out to Mal. My mother, ladies and gentlemen. From chiding to charming in zero seconds, flat. How does she do it? A true wonder.

"Mrs. Sanchez." Malachi took his time tucking his checkbook back into his suit. My mom stood there and waited the extra seconds, hand hanging in the air. Just when I thought he'd leave her like that forever, he grasped her fingers, then dropped them like she had a communicable disease.

"It's an honor. I'm such a fan of your work," she simpered.

I bit my lip to cover up a nervous laugh. She probably knew nothing about his work. But she knew he was famous, with apparently deep pockets. *One. Hundred. Thousand. Damn.* "I was looking forward to meeting you tonight. I didn't realize you'd be here with my daughter. Marija, you should have told us you'd be here. Your father could have found a way to seat you at our table."

Remarkable, honestly, how she made it sound like she wanted *me* at her table. Everyone, probably even the lady at the settlement desk, knew who she really wanted at her table.

"I asked Rija to come with me, as my date."

Good lord, Malachi sounded so cold. I was surprised my mom wasn't frozen to the spot. She blinked, her gaze turning sharp.

"I see. I didn't realize you and my daughter were so...close."

I hadn't given Sonia a hard time after it had taken her years to introduce me to Malachi. I understood the need to shelter the people you loved from the things that might pull you apart. In my case, my toxic-ass parents tended to chew people up and spit them back out again. It was why Sonia had only ever met them a handful of times, always in passing.

And why I had never, ever mentioned my relationship with Malachi to my parents.

"Mal is Sonia's brother, Mama," I supplied, keeping my response short. Sometimes that was best with her.

"And you've been friends for long?" Her stare honed into a needle prick of suspicion. Whenever she got her hands on me when Malachi wasn't around, it was going to be death by a thousand stinging accusations. Why didn't I tell them I was friends with a famous doctor? How long had this been going on? How could they use him to their greatest advantage?

"Friends, yes. Now, more." Malachi slid his hand down my arm, landing at my hip.

My mother's mouth popped open, eyes bugging.

"Rosa! There you are. People at the table are wondering where you got to."

As if this moment couldn't get any more awkward, my father rounded the corner. Dad's tux looked a little snug around his barrel of a chest. Gray peppered his thick mustache and slicked-back hair. Where mom was petite, dad was a skyscraper.

He used to carry me on his shoulders when I was little, and I'd felt like the tallest person in the world. Safe. Untouchable. Larger than life. My dad in a nutshell.

"Ah." His bluster dimmed when he saw me. Our relationship in a nutshell. "Marija. There you are. Quite the show you put on in front of a whole ballroom of my colleagues." His attention veered to Malachi, and I was all but forgotten. "Ah, Dr. Dobrev! Carl Sanchez, wonderful to meet you. Heard you're opening up a new clinic over on..."

"Wacker," my mother supplied. Of course, she'd already know where his office was. She'd probably been very busy sleuthing tonight when Mal had popped up on her radar. "Right on the loop."

"Swanky," Dad chuckled, eyeing Mal, gauging his reaction.

"My assistant will keep an office there for meetings and the corporate bullshit. The clinic is outside of the loop, where the people who actually need my services live." He swung his attention to me, eyes softening when he met mine. "We're finished here. Want to go home?"

"Um..." my gaze flickered between my parents. They had their best schmoozing faces on, battle-tested to keep a smile on their faces no matter what tea was spilled or what drama went down.

"Don't be silly! Marija, bring your friend over to our table. We'll find room for you." My mom smirked, probably already imagining the social coup of showing back up at her table with a celebrity.

It wasn't uncommon for me to join them at these things. Even after they'd cut me off financially years ago, and withheld their affection for years before that, I was often still expected to join them at the big dinners and fundraisers. God forbid someone think we were less than the perfect, happy medical family.

The problem was, I didn't want to go back to their stuffy little table and do a song and dance for their rich friends. I wanted to hightail it out of here and get Malachi out of his clothes as quickly as humanly possible.

Yet, even with such a powerful motivation to leave, I hesitated. When I'd become a nurse instead of a physician, they'd given up all hope that I'd live up to their ideal of what their daughter should be. Why would they continue to waste time and money on me when it was obvious I wasn't going to meet their astronomically high expectations?

I could still hear my father's voice, bellowing, *"My daughter will be a doctor, just like me! Just like my father before me! If you're not planning on becoming a physician...well, maybe you're not my daughter at all."*

Time and a good round of therapy (at Malachi's urging) had showed me it wasn't my fault that my parents found me lacking, and I couldn't concern myself with their feelings and reactions, when I was just trying to live the best life for me.

But, still...in our hearts, aren't we all just little kids who want to be loved by our parents? There was a small, timid part of me that couldn't help wanting to be that dutiful daughter, even now.

"Rija." Malachi's voice in my ear turned my head. My eyes connected with his and a heady mix of anger, support and...affection (love?) stared back at me. "I go where you go, Kitten."

Oh, fuck, did I love this man. Who else on this earth could deliver such a simple show of support, while also galvanizing my spine?

It was one thing for them to drag me around like a little doll. But I'd break into the lion enclosure and offer myself as a fresh sacrifice before letting them get their claws into Mal.

"We'll head out." I gave them a tight smile without making eye contact. "Enjoy the rest of the evening."

I'd barely stopped talking when Malachi whisked me away to the coat check. I fumbled in my clutch for my ticket and a few bucks for a tip. I could feel my parents' eyes on my back. Hushed whispers echoed in the hallway. They were conferring.

"Ah, yes, the lovely woman in red. Did you enjoy the party?" The attendant took my ticket while Mal did something on his phone. Calling a car, hopefully. Or booking two tickets to Tahiti. I'd have to go international to avoid the reckoning my parents would lay down the next time I saw them.

"Yes, it was lovely." I sounded so breathless, the man might not have even heard my response. My adrenaline was pumping, fight-or-flight kicking in. I'd been trained for nearly thirty years to do what my parents wanted. My body retaliated at my rebellion.

"Dinner, then? Soon? To celebrate your birthday." Mal set a bracing hand on my back at the sound of my mother's determined voice. "And you can bring your...friend." She sounded like it was a done deal.

"I'm, um, not sure, Mom. Let me get back to you." Avoidance was my friend. Easier to duck her ironclad will via text than in person.

"No, it'll have to be next week. Sunday. Your father and I are booked solid, but we can make that work."

"How fucking generous." Mal's voice was soft enough that it didn't carry to where my parents still stood by the settlement desk. I gave him a look. He gave me one right back before raising his voice, calling back to my mother without taking his eyes off me. "Rija is working on Sunday."

My mother scoffed at his words. "Rija leaves work at four. She can make time for a family dinner. I'll make Bandeja Paisa. All your favorites!"

"Tamales." Malachi finally turned to face them. Where was the coat check guy? I peered into the coat closet that was apparently Narnia. Anything to avoid my mother's eyes. She was like Medusa. She'd freeze me on the spot.

"What?"

"Your daughter's favorite Columbian food is tamales."

A pause. I swallowed, wrapping Mal's hand in mine, because this guy was facing Medusa head on and could still remember my favorite food.

"Of course, that's what I meant," Mom tittered.

"We'll see you both on Sunday." My dad's voice was firm. Final. Malachi took a breath, probably ready to fire back something scathing that would make me want to rip his tux off right here in this hallway. The protective thing he had going on here was *hot*.

But there, a beacon of hope in the darkness. My wrap.

"Yes, Sunday is fine. I'll text you to figure out the time. Thank you!" I grabbed my wrap from the attendant and shoved a few dollars in his hands. "Have a good night!" I chimed to the general hallway as I rushed towards the doors. The coat attendant, the cashier lady, my parents. Good night to all, and to all a good night. I wanted out of here. Now.

Chapter 8

"How are you folks doing tonight? Fancy looking party in there!" Our driver grinned at us from the front seat of the black car, a different man than the one who'd dropped me off. Thankfully, he'd been waiting in the Rover in front of the zoo so we could make a quick escape. I wouldn't put it past my mother to chase me down.

"Great party, yeah. Just happy to be heading home."

Thwump.

Mal slammed the car door behind us much harder than necessary. A storm cloud seemed to follow him into the dim interior. Our driver's brows jumped beneath his black ball cap.

"You good?" I reached over to rub Mal's arm. He'd been silent and tense during our walk to the car, and I couldn't help but feel guilty. The whole night we'd been floating in some sort of fairy tale, hands all over each other, finally *together*. And one run-in with my parents had ruined it all. "Mal, I'm sorry about—"

"Do not. Finish. That. Sentence." The air around him crackled with a type of angry energy I rarely saw from him. He was Dr. Do-Right. He preached patience, empathy, and understanding. Now, though, the muscles in his jaw clenched. "The only thing you should apologize for is how you...minimize yourself for them." He rocked back, flattening his body onto the seat as the car pulled away from the curb.

"Mal—"

"You are smart and vibrant and kind and beautiful. There is nothing about you that needs to be smaller. Nothing. Especially not for those people." His tone, his words, were so intense I had to look away. Our driver also averted his eyes as he wove into traffic, cranking the radio up a few dials to give us a semblance of privacy.

Mal sighed, reaching up to tangle one of my hands in his. "This is coming out all wrong. I'm not mad at you—"

"You're mad at them. I know. And I...appreciate that." *I love you for that. For standing by my side when I can't seem to get on my own two feet when my parents are around.* I bit my lip to keep the confession in, even though my heart was swelling up like a balloon.

He lifted our hands to his lips, brushing a kiss across my knuckles before resting our entwined fingers on his thigh. "I'm sorry. I didn't mean to snap at you."

"That's alright. It wasn't even a snap." Mal and I had been friends for two years, and our emotions tended to run hot around each other. It was hardly the first time one of us had gotten angry with the other.

My thumb stroked his wrist. I wanted to calm him and simultaneously assure myself that he was here and real and *mine*. I'd wanted him for so long, and now here he was, holding my hand like he'd never let go? Getting pissed off on my behalf and calling me vibrant? It felt like a dream. The confrontation with my parents slid to the back of my mind as I looked at him.

"I also didn't mean to slam the door so hard." Mal looked up at the driver. "Sorry about that."

Our driver waved him off. "All good, buddy."

"Yeah, all good," I echoed, rubbing my free hand against his arm, remembering the hundreds of times I'd wanted to do something similar and hadn't been able to. I relished it now. "Had some big feelings there, huh?"

He rolled his head to the side to give me a dry look. "I hate that they don't see you the way I see you. I know it hurts you, and that makes me want to murder them."

"Metaphorically, of course. Manslaughter is illegal."

"Murder, Kitten, implies intent. I would definitely intend it."

"Do we think talking about offing my parents is killing the mood a little bit? You know I'm down for a lot of things, but this might cross a line."

Mal grimaced, sliding his hand down his face before reaching over to smooth the fabric of my skirt over my thigh. A shimmer of heat followed where his fingers trailed. "I cannot believe I finally get to touch you and it's getting derailed by your fucking parents."

If only he knew. Maybe I had a lot of practice at compartmentalizing, or maybe I was just used to dealing with their demands, but either way, I was ready to move on to a different topic of conversation.

"Not derailed. I bet you can get us back on track."

Mal's dark eyes went nearly black, illuminated by the passing street lights. "Take your dress off and we'll see how well I can do."

As soon as the growled suggestion left his lips, an awkward, sputtering throat clearing sounded from the front of the car. I caught the driver's sheepish look in the rearview mirror while he turned the volume on the radio up a few more notches. Mal's hand scrubbed down his face again. Poor thing.

"Sorry," he murmured, leaning closer and lowering his voice. "That was out of line. Do you want to talk about it? Them? I know seeing them can throw you off, do you—"

I pressed a finger to his lips. They were so soft. There were hundreds, thousands of things I preferred he do with his mouth other than discuss the two people who hated me most in the world. "I don't want to talk about it. Yes, it was horrible timing to see them and yes, it threw me off. But that's a problem for tomorrow. Tonight," I slid our hands higher, brushing against the fly of his pants. "I don't want to think about that."

Tonight, after keeping my feelings—my lust—under lock and key for months, I didn't want to waste a single minute concentrating on anything other than *him*.

"Rija," Mal sighed, cupping my cheek. "You were very brave back there. I know how hard it must be to walk away from them like that. I love your strength."

"I am very strong. For instance, I can probably support my own body weight for a really long time, if we were to get into any adventurous positions back at your place."

His eyes closed and he whispered my name again, a fond admonishment slipping through the beginnings of his smile. "You're going to be the death of me. I'm going to have to bend you over the couch later."

Despite his quiet tone, our driver let out another strangled cough, cranking the dial on the radio again. I bit my lip, stifling a giggle at Mal's mortified look.

"Shit, I'm sorry. This is going all wrong," he whispered. I could just make it out over the music.

"It's not all wrong. Kiss me."

His eyes dropped to my mouth. The heat that had been steadily burning between us all night caught again. Every nerve ending in my body lit up in response to his thumb raking across my bottom lip.

"Not in public." Even as he said no, everything else about him said yes. The way he leaned closer, the way his fingers squeezed mine even more. The quick, almost imperceptible uptick of his breath.

"We're not in public, and that guy already knows you plan on bending me over the couch later." I paused for a beat, tongue darting out to lick the pad of his thumb. He was close to me, leaning over into my space. I heard him groan, even over the music. "Couch, huh? Interesting choice."

"Couch is..." he swallowed, shifting in his seat. A quick glance down confirmed he was sporting an impressive erection. My blood pulsed hot. Tonight, it was all for me. I'd get to touch him, feel him. Suddenly, that was all that mattered. "Couch is like fourth choice."

"I want to hear your top three." My leg slid over his knee, allowing me to sink further into him. The closer I got, the closer I wanted to be. A few more inches and I'd practically be in his lap.

"Bed," he rasped, leaning closer to drag his nose along my jaw. Goosebumps raised on my legs. "Shower. Balcony. I'll make you come while you're looking out at the...city..."

His words echoed in the split-second of dead air before the radio rolled into the next beat.

Our driver winced, looking as uncomfortable as Mal did. "Only so much I can do in between the songs, man."

A cackle of laughter burst out of me before I stifled it with my hand over my mouth.

While my body shook, I felt Mal plant his hands on my hips and haul me across the leather bench seat, pushing me as far away as I could get. I was so wound up over him, I'd forgotten about seatbelts.

"I'm so sorry. I'm not usually like this," Malachi assured our driver, pointing a finger at me when I tried to scoot back towards the middle. "You! Stay over there. I can't think when you're..." His fingers rippled in my direction, "there."

On his side of the car, Mal's face was beet-red, chest heaving. I made a big show of clicking my seatbelt around my torso. Only for the car to slow to a stop in front of my apartment building.

Or, now, our apartment building.

As of today, Mal had officially moved in upstairs. I sank my teeth into my lip as I climbed out of the car, trying to keep a massive grin from spreading over my face. I peered up at floors and floors of sleek glass and concrete while Mal leaned over the passenger window to talk with the driver.

Mal lived here now, just an elevator ride away. The thought sent a shiver of excitement down my spine. Soon, Sonia would be back in Chicago and we could tell her that things had...changed between us. Because they would. Soon. Tonight. Right now.

I wondered how fast that elevator could go.

"You." Mal turned to glare at me, stuffing something into his breast pocket while the Rover rolled away into the night. He gave me that warning finger again. The stare. The voice. Yet, his eyes were hot, mouth quirked in the sexiest smile I'd ever seen. "You are nothing but trouble. How come you climb all over me and I'm the one who looks like a degenerate?"

"You are a degenerate. For me," I purred, tip-toeing closer. Oh, my God, we were so close to my apartment. His apartment. Anyone's apartment! In, like, five minutes flat, I was going to be fully naked with Malachi Dobrev. My little heart couldn't take it. It was hammering so hard, people could probably see my throbbing pulse up in space.

Barring the unfortunate encounter with my parents, the night had been perfect. How he'd held me, the way our hands were never far from each other. Touching him, being with him, calling him mine...it was everything I'd dreamed of for so long. I even loved that there was a random driver somewhere in the city who knew we couldn't keep our hands off each other.

I was done waiting. I wanted him now.

"Come on, Kitten." His voice was jagged, gaze so hot, I knew he was thinking the same. He offered me his palm. It was warm and strong as it enveloped mine. "Hands only," he ground out, pulling me inside and towards the elevators. We passed by two of the building's security guards in a rush. "I don't need some security video of me ripping your dress off showing up on TMZ."

"Because it's bad for your sensitive, respectful image?"

"Because I'm the only one who gets to see your tits."

I was used to his words, of course. He used them on me all the time when he was trying to make me come. Now, with his apartment only a few seconds away, hearing him say something like that took hot to a whole new level.

"Malachi." I whispered as the elevator doors shut, enclosing us together. The car felt sweltering. Sweat shone on Mal's brow. I wasn't the only one feeling the heat.

"One-six-five-zero," he murmured, staring at my mouth.

"Huh...?" Had I forgotten how to speak English? Was my brain melting in a puddle of wanton lust? I stepped closer the second he slid away to the corner of the elevator. If it weren't for the hand he raised between us, I would have already jumped him.

Mal cleared his throat, gaze raking down my dress. "One-six-five-zero. I live in the penthouse. You need a code to get in. Can you remember that?" He dragged his eyes away from me with visible effort, keying the code into the pad and pressing the P button. My stomach lurched as the car rose.

"I won't remember that." I was too busy mentally licking his throat. My feet, without any direction from my brain, stepped closer. My gold heels clicked on the elevator tile.

"You should stay over there, Kitten." Even as he said it, the hand he held between us flexed, reaching for me, grasping, as if his body was no longer under his control, either. His fingers were hot, nearly scorching. Or maybe that was just the insane attraction between us, fizzing on our skin like a chemical reaction. We were going to be explosive.

"I don't want to stay over here anymore."

"Then don't." He pulled me closer. The lapels of his jacket slid against my chest. He was wearing too many layers. My fingers slipped inside, smoothing over the starched fabric of his shirt. His heart was beating as quickly as mine.

"You're very agreeable." My hand worked lower, undoing the buttons of his jacket. Peeling away at least one of those layers.

"I'm weak. Anything you want, Rija. Anything." His head ducked down closer, breath blowing the loose curls at my shoulders.

As the elevator chimed and he backed me out of it, all I could see were his onyx eyes gleaming in the dim light of the apartment. I didn't pause to look at the room around me, the floor, his new place.

He was sucking up all my attention. All my oxygen, even. I barely had time to draw in a gasp when my shoulder blades came up against a wall.

And then Malachi Dobrev was kissing me the way I'd wanted him to for months. Years, even. He didn't go slowly. At the first brush, his lips ravished mine, tongue demanding entrance into my mouth. He groaned when I granted it. The first taste of him on my lips nearly buckled my knees.

Malachi. Malachi. Malachi. His name was a chant in my head. The only thing my poor, delirious synapses and brain cells could hold on to while every brush of his mouth reverberated throughout my body.

"Christ, Rija," he cursed into my mouth, his gratuitous, satisfied moan like fresh air in my lungs. We'd both been waiting for this for too long. We fell on each other like we were ravenous. My fingers speared into his hair, gripped his jaw. He tilted for me as he pulled my hips closer, slanting more of his mouth across mine. His tongue thrust harder inside, lapping.

I arched, and we both groaned at the feel of my breasts pressing against his chest. He was so hard, muscled everywhere that I was soft and pliant. A perfect fit, like I'd always known we'd be.

"I need..." He grunted, pulling the strap of my dress down, the loose fabric gave way easily to his onslaught. His breath caught when my breast spilled free. He stared, as enchanted as I was at the sight of his palm cupping the soft weight. His fingers were dark against my pale skin. Callouses rasped against the sensitive mound.

"Mal, please," I whimpered. My fingers closed around his, lifting, offering. Needing. How many nights had I laid awake thinking about his hands on my breasts? His mouth?

His breath caught while he lunged down to suck the hardened nub into his mouth, as if I'd said the thought out loud. The hot, sweet pull of his lips speared pure pleasure through me, sending heat straight between my legs, making me cry out.

He moaned at the sound, pulling away and looking at me with wild, crazed eyes. His pupils were blown, mouth open to suck down heaving breaths before he was on me again. Lips on lips, so perfect and hot and *right* that I nearly cried out again.

"Fuck."

I'd hardly registered his curse before his palm wrapped around the back of my thighs and suddenly I was airborne.

"Fuck!" I repeated, the squeaking peal of my voice a ridiculous contrast to his low growl. My arms looped around his neck as he pounded, purposeful, down the hall.

I caught a brief glimpse of a massive living room, boxes and furniture strewn around. The blown glass pendant lights over the kitchen island were on, casting a warm, orangey glow over the place.

"That's the idea, yes." His fingers clenched on my ass, supporting me with one arm while he tore at his shirt buttons with the other. It was a breathtaking show of coordination, not to mention strength. I was happy with my body but...I wasn't exactly hitting up the guest room/pilates studio on a daily basis.

"Mal, you're going to drop me." White walls sped by in my periphery on one side, the twinkling lights of Chicago on the other. How big was this place? He ducked through a doorway.

"Yes," he agreed again. And then I was free-falling, reeling for the half-second it took for my back to hit the mattress. By the time I'd scrambled to my elbows, Mal's shirt was off and he was working on his pants. "Get naked, Kitten. Now. Please."

His "please" was an afterthought, squeezed out on the tail end of his rushed, desperate words. It made me grin, even as I reached back towards my zipper with trembling hands. This was happening, this was happening, right now. I was *in his bedroom* and this was happening.

The zipper slid down. I yanked the straps down my shoulders and stood.

His hands stilled on his own clothes, eyes blazing. As the dress slid down my body, collapsing in a fall of red silk to pile at my feet on the wood floor, his eyes snapped across my skin. Neck, breasts, stomach, thighs.

Then his hands were on me, hauling me to him. We both gasped. The feel of his body against mine was overwhelming. After so long merely imagining what he'd feel like against me, the reality was almost more than I could handle.

Heat swept through me, following wherever his hands roamed. He was rough and reverent. The contrast was yet another detail that overloaded my brain. I knew he could be sweet. I knew he could be rough. I hadn't realized he could be both at the same time.

The only thing I could do was reciprocate, lavishing him with my touch. I was greedy, clutching and grabbing, running hungry fingers across the defined muscles of his stomach, his arms, his jaw.

"Rija, your hands on me..." He groaned, the sound cut off when his mouth met mine again, his sucking pulls echoing between my legs. Another wave of pleasure made me shiver, more slickness flooding. Our hands were feverish. Everywhere all at once—arms tangling, lips and teeth and heat.

Maybe we'd go out like this. Together, in a blaze of desire.

He palmed my ass, bunching the soft fabric of my seamless panties. "Off," he whispered into my mouth.

"You too," I gasped, my hand reaching down into his open pants. His groan sounded pained, hands shaking just as much as mine as he shoved his pants and briefs down in one swift move. I wrapped my fingers around his length. *Finally.*

He was soft and steel-hard. I pumped once down to the root before his hand caught my wrist.

"Fuck. Fuckfuckfuckfuckfuckfuckfuck." He pushed me gently back onto the bed. I bounced when I sat, eyeing the expanse of his chest in front of me. "Fuck," he repeated when I licked up the center. He tasted like salt and limes.

"This is going to be fast." His words were glass over gravel, voice harsh and glittering as he pulled my underwear down.

When he found my center, I jerked, a full-body spasm. "Yes! Yes, please. Fast."

He groaned, fingers gliding up and down, aided by the overflowing wetness of my slit. "So, so fast. I'm sorry, Kitten." Even as he apologized, he shoved my legs apart, climbing higher to line his cock up where I needed him. The first brush of the head against me nearly made me come. I cried out, struggling to pull air into my body.

We were going too fast, too slow. I wanted it to last forever. I wanted it to be over *now* so I could know what it felt like to come with him touching me, inside me.

He groaned, burying his head in the crook of my neck as he slid inside an inch at a time. I was so wet, he entered easily. Still, he pulled back once, slid in further.

And it was over. The stretch, the delicious feel of his skin against mine, the mind-blowing pleasure of it all, months and months of needing his hands on me. All of it crystalized at once, then fragmented. His name exploded from my lips in a scream, toes curling as my orgasm ripped through me. I couldn't breathe. I couldn't see. I could only feel.

Him, above me, hips pumping in and out. My core twisted, legs gripping his hips as he rode me through my climax. It crested in a wildfire. All I could do was jerk and shudder and moan when his fingers reached down to rub my clit.

The rushing in my ears subsided, though my body was still riding the high he fueled. I was still coming. Or maybe he just felt that good inside me. An eternal orgasm.

"So good, Ri. Don't want it to stop." He abandoned my clit, gripping my thigh, holding me open as his hips snapped against mine faster and faster. "Wanted this for so long, Kitten."

"Malachi," I mewled, still drowning in the feeling of his body.

He groaned, eyes meeting mine. "My name. Say it again, Ri. While I fuck you."

"Malachi," I gasped, again and again. He thrust so hard I inched up the mattress. He looped his arm around my waist, hanging onto me.

He looked pained, panting. "Rija, it's...everything." His eyes squeezed shut, and he came with a shout. His thrusts turned jerky, spearing me in a primal, unconscious rhythm that set me off again. I screamed, pussy gripping him, pulling at the warm pulses I felt inside me.

He kept pumping, groaning my name and how good it was and gibberish I somehow still understood about him and me and us and *perfect*. Finally, he slowed, grunting and panting while he still slid in and out of my sensitive folds, like he couldn't bring himself to stop. I didn't want him to. Even while my body came down from my high, my muscles starting to protest how tightly I was wrapped around him, I wanted him again.

He groaned my name, ragged, as he finally collapsed over me, holding his weight on his elbows.

His breath was hot against my collarbone, chest heaving in time with mine. Even in this incredible aftermath, the feel of him against me, his skin on mine, felt like a miracle. My hands couldn't stop moving against him, roaming the broad expanse of his back, cradling his face while I pressed my lips across his hairline.

After another moment, he rolled to his side, pulling me with him. We both winced when he slid out. He stroked a hand down my face.

"Was I too rough? I felt like I couldn't control—"

"It was perfect." I pressed my lips against his, the chaste pecks turning into long, leisurely kisses. He hummed when I pressed closer to him, tangling my leg between his. "It was perfect, Mal."

His forehead rested against mine. We stayed like that while our breathing evened and my mind spun around the fact that I was here with him, like this.

He lay next to me, seemingly as dazed as I was. At one point, he started whispering about getting a towel to clean me up, only to settle back onto the bed, tucking the sheets around us when I begged him not to leave. I felt like I couldn't be parted from him for a second.

I must have dozed. The next thing I knew, I was arching into his stroking fingers on my neck.

"I'm sorry, Kitten. I need you again."

I smiled while he covered my face in kisses. "Don't apologize."

"Are you sore?" His hand was already traveling down my body, pausing to brush against my tightening nipples. When he reached the spot between my legs, he found the wetness still there, easing his way in. He was so gentle, stroking softly.

"Not sore enough."

Our eyes met in the dark, the city lights outside the window illuminating us. He swallowed, a smile tried to draw across his lips and didn't quite make it. "Sounds like a challenge."

I swept a lock of hair back from his forehead, arching. Already he was rolling us, fitting himself at my entrance. "More like a request," I murmured, gasping at the feel of him pressing inside.

The need I felt for him defied logic. How could I want him this much, like I was dying for him, when I'd just been sleeping in his arms? The stark hunger on his face reflected my own feelings back at me. His eyes were edged with something like wariness or acceptance.

"Rija." My name whispered from his lips, but I heard more than just my name. When he eased in and out, careful, despite my telling him I wasn't hurt, I felt more than just the friction of his cock inside me. When he finally moaned, breaking his gentle pumping for faster, feverish fucking, there was more than just desire rising up from my core.

I bit my lip to stop it from spilling out. The love I had for this man, the incredible, incandescent alive-ness I felt from being in his arms. It flowed from my eyes instead, and I came with tears streaming down my face. He kissed them away, murmuring my name and beautiful nonsense and how he felt it, too.

Chapter 9

"Malachi?"

He was a hard sleeper. Uncovering such an intimate quirk made me smile. A deeply satisfied feeling settled into my chest that had nothing to do with the multiple orgasms last night.

I'd been whispering his name and running my hands over the dips and valleys of his muscled chest for over a minute, and so far his only reaction had been to grunt in his sleep, roll towards me, and scoop me up in his arms.

Even while he was asleep, he held me tightly, like he, too, was enjoying the feel of our bodies pressed together. It was early, too early, and the morning sun was just peeking over the horizon, but the huge floor-to-ceiling windows flooded everything with light.

It was annoying to be woken so early, but on the plus side, I got to lie in the massive, cozy bed and stare at him like a creeper for a few more minutes. As the room brightened just a bit more, I mentally added "buy curtains" to my to-do list. But that could wait. I had something more pressing on my mind.

"Mal," I whispered louder, indulging in a longer sweep of my palm down his abs. He was a work of art.

"Need to re-hydrate if you want it again," he grumbled against my neck, pulling me closer.

"No, this is more important than that."

His breath fluttered against my clavicle, slow and steady.

"Mal?"

He grunted.

"Where the fuck is my dog?"

His eyes popped open.

***

"It's seven a.m."

"I know, I'm sorry. It was a reunion emergency."

Adam, Mal's PA and publicist, shrugged off Mal's apology. "I was already up. I just don't think you've ever called me this early on a weekend before, except for the security—" He faltered, looking at me and back to Mal.

"What security?" I asked, filling the silence that was very abrupt and very awkward. Even Siggy stopped chewing on the rope toy I held for him, eyes flicking around all the humans in the room.

Yesterday, Sigmund had stayed in a well-appointed hotel suite with Adam while Mal moved in and attended the gala. But I'd woken hungry for pancakes, Mal, and my dog. Not necessarily in that order. Mal had now fulfilled two out of three requests. Our pancake order should be ready any moment for pickup.

"Just some issues that have popped up with the new building." Mal knelt, giving Siggy's ears a rub. "Alarms, codes."

Adam loosed a breath through puffed cheeks. "Yeah. Codes."

I didn't miss the look he gave Mal, or how Mal ignored it. I chalked it up to business drama and the second I was sitting on Mal's new, kajillion square foot balcony overlooking the city, pancakes syrup'd and Siggy chasing a ball around, I forgot about it altogether.

Sunday

"It has occurred to you that I can't just wear your old gym clothes for the rest of my life, right?" I pulled at the oversized shirt dripping from my body. We'd just gotten back from Sigmund's morning walk, and the only clothes I had here—a very wrinkled silk gown—hadn't seemed appropriate for the task. Seeing as we'd barely left the apartment in the last twenty-four hours, it wasn't a huge deal, especially because Malachi seemed to take immense pleasure in seeing me in his clothes.

But still, someone had to think about the logistics, here.

"Has it occurred to you that you don't have to wear anything at all for the rest of your life? Think of how much time it would save."

I rolled my eyes, grinning when his hands snuck up the shirt, making a beeline for my breasts. I still wasn't used to the possessive, high-handed way he touched me. As if he was entitled to it. I loved it. "I'm sure my patients would be very cool about that. Not to mention my boss."

He hummed, licking my throat. "Quit your job. Stay here and be my sex slave. I'll buy you nice tequila and feed you tapas every night."

"He makes a compelling argument," I muttered to Siggy, who was ignoring us in favor of a chew toy he'd just wrestled from under the couch. I tilted my head back so Mal could place nipping bites along my jaw. "But then there will be the inevitable boredom. The lack of personal fulfillment. Resentment that you've taken me from a career I love. Screaming, yelling, division of assets. Etcetera, etcetera."

Mal pulled back to look at me, brow raised. I wanted to smooth my fingers over it. "The demise of our relationship is *'etcetera, etcetera?'*"

"Only if you don't let me go grab a few tank tops and my own toothpaste."

He'd graciously gifted me a brand new toothbrush yesterday morning that he proudly displayed in the cup next to his, but I hated his toothpaste. What psycho liked cinnamon?

He sighed, looking at my neck and the wet marks still there. "Fine. Meet you down there."

***

"It's me." A jingle of a collar accompanied Mal's voice. "And Sigmund."

"Siggy!" I called. The pup took the corner into my room hard, skidding on the gray linoleum in his rush to get to me. I scooped him into my arms, my heart filling up at his wiggly enthusiasm. He acted like it had been days since he'd seen me, not just twenty minutes.

"I'm almost done," I hollered into the hall where Mal was following my dog at a more normal speed.

"Really?" I could hear his incredulity before he even entered the room.

"Yes." I gestured to my duffel bag, already mostly full on the bed. I'd already packed essential toiletries. Now I was just quibbling over how many pairs of leggings to bring, which was ridiculous, because I would be back down here to get ready for work tomorrow morning. Plus, if I needed anything, I was just a short elevator ride away.

"You're joking." He glared at my duffel like he wanted to eviscerate it. I automatically held Siggy closer to my chest. Maybe Mal had really only expected me to bring a single change of clothes? I didn't want to be too presumptuous, but the way things had been going the last few days, it seemed like he wanted to keep me around for a while...

Maybe I'd misread the situation.

"It's just essentials," I assured him. When I looked between his scowl and my bag, my stomach clenched up, but I kept talking, ignoring the uncomfortable sensation. This was *Malachi* I was talking to. I had always been myself around him and I wouldn't stop now, even if there was more on the line than there used to be.

"And, alright, maybe it's more than *you* need," I babbled, "but I'm a high maintenance woman, and if that's a problem...why are you shaking your head?"

He disappeared into the hallway, coming back a second later with a stack of three massive cardboard moving boxes. I recognized them because we'd been methodically unpacking dozens of them around his apartment over the course of the last two days.

"Kitten." Something in his voice froze me. My eyes snapped to his as if he'd ordered them to. He leaned against the door frame, sexy as sin, and gave me a challenging look. "Pack like you're never coming back."

Monday

"What happened to the sex slave idea?"

Mal had been awake by the time I'd made it back into his bedroom...our bedroom?...with an espresso for him.

"As lovely as that idea seems at—" I checked my smartwatch "—five thirty in the morning on a Monday, I'll remind you once more about the resentment and lack of personal fulfillment."

"Right. That." He accepted the cup from my hands, watching as I twisted my hair into a clip and applied some moisturizer in the dim lights of the bathroom. I hadn't been worried about waking him, now that I knew he was a heavy sleeper, but I may have cursed the espresso machine in at least two different languages and one made up one. I hadn't been quiet about it, but neither had the machine when it spit and hissed back at me.

"Coffee machine give you any trouble?" Like he could read my mind, he piped up from the bed. I refused to meet his gaze in the mirror as Siggy jumped up to snuggle into his lap. Lucky dog.

"No. All good." I tried to sound breezy, but perhaps some of my latent anger leaked through. Out of the corner of my eye, I thought I caught him smirking.

"Tutorial didn't stick?"

"Considering yesterday's espresso tutorial got derailed halfway through and we ended up sullying the coffee bar for all time, we should all just be impressed I got anything to come out of it."

Mal and his coffee. He was such a snob. He'd been handling coffee for the last two days, executing the perfect vanilla latte for me as soon as I woke. His machine was a monster. Italian and complicated and shiny, so I'd been happy to leave him on barista duty this weekend.

But I couldn't expect him to cater to me on days like today, when I was leaving so early for the hospital. And it would be nice, sometimes, for me to make the coffee for him. He worked so hard and was so perfect and gave me *so many orgasms*. He deserved it.

"I am impressed. It's delicious."

"You're just saying that." I padded to him and leaned over the bed. He willingly tilted his cup to give me a sip. I considered it as the brew swirled in my mouth.

"Not bad, I guess. I'll get better with practice."

His eyes dropped to my lips. I tilted forward for a kiss, easy, comfortable, like we'd done this every day for years.

"Come on," he leaned away, setting his cup on the nightstand. "I'll walk you out."

Between walking Siggy and bouts of very energetic sex, we'd worked a little magic on his new apartment. Most of the boxes were unpacked. We'd spent yesterday afternoon grunting and sweating, moving furniture around his living room until it was just the way we wanted it.

Then spent the evening grunting and sweating *on* the furniture.

His cream sectional and navy pillows looked inviting against the backdrop of his massive windows. We'd ordered curtains for some of the rooms, but those wouldn't get in till later this week. A huge print of the Rocky mountains broke up some of the white monotony of the hallway. We'd made good headway on his office. His...our?...bedroom was done. Even my extra leggings were folded neatly, looking ridiculous by themselves on an empty half of the closet that he'd refused to put his things on. Mine, I supposed.

I hugged Sigmund to me while I walked to the front door, grabbing my work bag. I'd only been here for two days and it already felt more like home than anywhere else I'd ever lived. My heart hurt to walk out the doors and leave it.

"It's stupid how much I don't want you to leave right now." Mal read my mind again. We paused by the front door. We'd need some shelves here. Hooks for bags. A little bowl for keys.

I sighed. "I'm thinking the same thing, trust me." I rubbed my cheek against Siggy's head and set him down. Mal put his arms around me. Maybe the apartment felt like home, but *this* felt like...finding a part of myself I hadn't known was missing.

"I'll be back a little after four."

"And we'll be here, a little before four, whining at the door while we wait."

The image he conjured made me grin. I leaned in to kiss his cheek. "You don't have to leave your office early for me. I'll hang out here till you get home from work."

At four-twenty-seven, I walked in the door to find Siggy, tail wagging so hard his body shuddered, and Mal, doing an equally ridiculous and excited shimmy while holding a gorgeous bouquet of flowers.

Wednesday

"What do you think about this?" We were watching TV in his bedroom, new curtains pulled closed to block out the lights of the city, curled up on his California King and scrolling through our phones every once in a while. Millennial heaven.

I glanced at his screen to see a large, antique-looking wooden apothecary cabinet. Round, blown-glass knobs glittered on each of the dozens of little, square drawers.

"That's nice. What's it for?"

His chin jutted toward a box in the closet. One of the only ones we'd yet to unpack. The one he'd personally packed, himself, kneeling on my bedroom floor and rolling each toy in clean bubble wrap. Nestling them carefully into the cardboard. "The collection, of course."

I'd told him he was being ridiculous. We didn't even need the toys. Not with all the action we were making ourselves. Yes, I was sore now and no, that didn't slow us down at all. But he'd insisted, hovering protectively over the massive box of vibrators with a tragic look on his face. "Rija, they're family."

Needless to say, the vibrators had made the trek with me to the upper floors.

Still, it was one thing to box them up for sentimental reasons and keep them in the closet. This was another thing altogether.

"You want to *house* the collection? In its own...furniture?"

"I told you I'd give you a dresser."

I blinked at him, then back down at the phone. "You...I...you can't buy me a dresser for my vibrators."

He looked at me like I was insane. "I can buy you vibrators, but you draw the line at storage?"

"It's..." I floundered, not sure why I felt so taken aback by his suggestion. Maybe because him *literally* buying me a dresser for his place seemed like a big step for us to be taking so casually. Even though we'd moved three boxes of clothes and stuff from my apartment up here, I still technically lived downstairs, with Sonia, who we still hadn't told about our new situation. She was too busy living it up in New York, and we were too busy in heaven.

Or maybe I balked because the toys had been our dirty little secret for so long. It boggled my mind that he wanted to make a place especially for them, not shove them in the back of the closet or an empty drawer. He wasn't just making room for them; he was creating a whole space for them.

"Talk to me, Sanchez. You don't like it?" He cocked his head, patient. Curious.

"No, I do...It's pretty much perfect, actually..." It was. I could already envision it in the room, right there by the closet. It was gorgeous and had a price tag that spoke to its craftsmanship.

"Pretty much?"

"Well..." I blinked back down at the picture. "Is it too big? I don't think I have that many."

He scoffed. "Kitten, just because I'm sleeping with you doesn't mean you stop getting presents." He navigated to the checkout page. "We'll fill this up. Maybe we should get two."

Laughter sputtered out of me because it was the only defense I had for the surge of feelings breaking through the surface of my chest and blocking out rational thought. "Oh, really?"

"It's called having your cake and eating it, too."

I called it being in love with an amazing man who somehow knew what I wanted before I did and made me feel more cherished and important than anyone in the world ever had.

But we'd only just started touching last week. Regardless of our history together, it felt too soon to rocket to the next step like that. I'd been waiting *months* for this. To just lay in bed, wrapped up in his arms, doing nothing.

So, I had no words for him. Certainly not the ones I wanted to say. I ended up tackling him, instead, and riding him until the only words he had were my name.

Thursday

"What's the point of having your own business if you can't play hooky?"

Mal looked up from a dusty desk, grinning. "What are you doing here?"

He'd tried to stay home since I had the day off, but more emergencies kept popping up, and he hadn't been able to swing it.

I dangled a takeout bag in his direction. "Hungry?"

He rounded the desk, pulling me into his arms for a kiss. "You brought me lunch?"

"Well, everyone's...gotta eat, right?" I managed to get out around his seeking lips.

He pulled back, eyes darting back and forth between mine. Something in his expression made me pause. He was tense. Nervous? That tightness clamped around my stomach, accompanied by a voice in my head telling me I had overstepped. Done too much. *Been* too much. Again.

"Is that okay? I can just drop it and run if yo—"

I didn't get a chance to finish before his mouth was on mine again. He kissed me urgently, like one of us was about to board a plane. It felt desperate, and not in a good way. I pulled back, stroking the line between his brows. "Hey, what's wrong?"

"Nothing." He nuzzled his nose into my neck. "Nothing, just... work stuff."

"More moving crises?"

"Mmm," he nodded, hands circling around to the small of my back. I spread my fingers through his hair, guilt pricking at me.

"I'm sorry. I can't help feel a little responsible. I mean, you're kind of moving here for me, and it's been nothing but drama."

He pulled out of my grasp, hands on my shoulders, eyes more serious than I'd ever seen them. "This is not your fault. Never think that. Ever, alright? I made this choice for me. For us. You are not causing these...issues."

"O-okay..." I stuttered. He studied me, like he wanted to make sure his point sunk in. "Alright. I'll stop feeling bad."

"Good. Good." His eyes went hazy. Even though he was looking at me, I got the feeling he wasn't fully present.

"Do you want to talk about it? It seems like this is starting to really weigh you down."

His head shook. "No. I actually don't want to think about this at all. I want to have lunch with a beautiful woman and think about other stuff."

I hesitated. He hadn't shared any specifics of what was going on with his clinic. The building around us was beautiful. It was still being renovated, as the plaster dust and construction equipment could attest to, but shaping up. I could visualize it—the cozy, classy atmosphere would put people at ease here. A place of respite. Self-reflection. It seemed like it was all coming along fine. All the workers moved like a well-oiled machine. Adam had winked at me from his desk out front.

Nothing seemed like it was on fire, but every night this week, Mal had come home with knots in his shoulders, tense until I could get him to wind down.

Still, if he wanted a break, I could provide it. I held the takeout bag up. "I've got the lunch and the woman. What do you want to talk about?"

I squeaked when he swept me off my feet and hauled me up against his desk with a smile.

Friday

Mal drew the line at Siggy sleeping in the bed with us. He said he'd waited too long to have me all to himself to share me, even with the dog. Plus, Siggy wasn't house-trained yet. I conceded both points were valid, even though I hated to miss out on his warm puppy snuggles.

On days I didn't go to work before the sun came up, Mal took Siggy down to the apartment courtyard to do his morning business, then let him wriggle into bed with me.

Yesterday, Siggy and I had snoozed together in the Egyptian cotton sheets for a few hours after Mal had gone to work, taken a long walk around the city, and then hung out on the balcony for most of the afternoon.

An almost perfect day, really. Just missing Mal. And Sonia. I hadn't gone this long without her in a long time. It didn't help that I'd had to sprint back down to our apartment twice this week to return her FaceTime calls. I couldn't risk her getting suspicious, not when she'd only been gone for two weeks.

Mal and I would start soft-launching our relationship with her soon. Like he'd said, pictures together, maybe a mention of a dinner out on our group thread. Every time I thought about it, my heart sank like a stone, the familiar, guilty feeling roiling in my stomach. That queasy sensation doubled whenever I realized that sometimes, I was too caught up in Mal to feel guilty, at all.

I could only hope that when all this went down, she'd be understanding. Angry, at first, probably, but...hopefully she'd come around. I couldn't think about the alternative.

Mal softly lifting Siggy out of his crate had woken me early. The thought of my best friend, and the potential consequences of my actions with her brother, had kept me from drifting back to sleep.

The bedroom door opened, and Siggy wiggled into bed next to me, as he had yesterday. Today, though, Mal slid back under the covers, too. He gathered both me and the dog in his arms.

"Hey, Dr. Do-Right. You gotta work today." I reminded him, turning to snuggle deeper into him, Siggy burrowing between us. Maybe we could squeeze in a few more minutes like this. Our little family.

"Mmmm, what if I just don't?"

I laughed, tracing the sprinkling of hair on his chest. "If you don't go into work, who's going to look pretty in front of the camera? Those TikToks don't make themselves, you know."

"Sure, but as someone very wise and gorgeous and fucking sexy once told me, '*what's the point of having your own business if you can't play hooky?*'"

I pulled back, laughing when Siggy squirmed in between us to rest his nose on the pillow. But Mal wasn't laughing. His eyes crinkled at the corners in a hint of a smile, but he looked too serious to pull it off.

All week, he'd come home with a weight pressing on him. He tried to hide it, but I could tell how much this move was taking a toll on him. Maybe even his business.

"Are you going to tell me what's wrong?" I ran my fingers across the lines etching his forehead. He avoided the question and my gaze by ducking to nuzzle his face into my shoulder.

"Mal?"

His breath blew hot against my skin, and sounded like surrender. "I'm just tired, Ri." His nose brushed back and forth over my skin. "Everything is so up in the air. I just...want a break. Even if it's for a day."

When he finally looked up at me, his dark lashes framed pleading eyes. "I don't wanna go to work." He pouted, but that quiet resignation still hung around him like a thundercloud.

"Things are really that bad?" Malachi Dobrev never gave up. On anything. Even if it was only for a day. He'd be the first to tell his patients that they needed to practice self-care and slow down if they needed it, but his fatal flaw was his dogged determination to save the world, or die trying. I'd never seen him like this before.

"Just...things that need time. Things out of my control." His forehead pressed into my shoulder once more.

I shuttled my fingers through his hair. "My poor little perfectionist. Finally found something you can't manage into submission by sheer force of will?" I teased, hoping to get a smile out of him. His only response was to press a kiss against my skin. I waited another moment, my fingers gliding through his hair.

"It'll be okay, Mal," I whispered, pressing my lips to the crown of his head. A sigh shuddered out of him again.

"You don't mind if I crash your off day?"

I could hardly hear him, he was pressed so tightly into me. I frowned down at him, wondering where my confident, assured boyfriend had gone? Maybe distraction was the key.

"Hmm. Actually, you might be able to help me out. See, I had 'give someone a blowjob' on my to-do list today, so I'm looking for a volunteer. Any chance you'd be interested?"

His head rose enough to meet my gaze. His face looked hot and dark. Progress.

"Sigmund, go to your crate," Mal ordered, his eyes flicking down to the dog when he didn't move an inch from the pillow. They stared at each other. "Siggy. Crate."

Mal snapped his fingers and Siggy finally hopped up with a grumbling whine, jumping off the bed to settle into his crate. A good trick. We'd been working on it all week.

"I think I can be of service," Mal growled. I grinned at him, already sinking beneath the covers.

"I think I'm the one doing the servicing here, actually."

He groaned.

Chapter 10

I was on edge Sunday, dreading having to call my mother during my lunch break. Mal had promised he'd come with me to the dinner she'd been texting me about all week, but I couldn't do that to him. I'd stick with my original plan: tell mom something came up with Mal's work, and weather the storm tonight, solo.

I wasn't looking forward to it, but I'd handled my parents' disappointments countless times now. Besides, the thought of coming home and cozying up to Mal and Siggy afterwards made it seem less daunting. Somewhat.

I never enjoyed getting on my mother's bad side, and I already had a pit in my stomach when I stepped out of the scrub room.

"Sanchez, I need you to come with me." My sneakered feet stumbled to a halt in the hallway outside of the OR. Dr. Caplan, the director at Cedar's cardiothoracic surgery unit, stood in front of me looking serious.

The pit in my stomach ripped open into a chasm.

"Is everything alright?" I gulped, mind racing over the last few days. Had I done something wrong? In my Mal-induced haze, had I made some horrible mistake?

The look he gave me didn't ease my sudden spike of anxiety. He seemed apologetic, but uneasy? "Let's discuss it in my office."

Adrenaline rushed through my veins. Megan, one of the surgical assistants, passed by, her eyes asking if everything was okay. I shook my head, unsure of the answer. "Well, I...I have to eval this patient..." I looked back at the OR, where just minutes ago, I'd been going about my regular day, assisting with a bypass surgery.

"I've already asked LeeAnn to step in on that." Caplan motioned me forward. "Come with me, please."

It was surreal, riding in the elevator silently with Caplan. Despite what my parents might think, I'd always been good. Good student, good worker. I'd never once been called into the principal's office, or anything.

I didn't know what to say. Was I supposed to say something? I continued to wrack my brain. What was going on? When I asked again, Caplan just shook his head and told me we'd discuss it in his office.

We walked down the hallway in a grim silence, my palms sweating. Fuck, I'd have to cancel dinner plans with my parents. There was no way I'd be able to face them if I was getting fired. My mouth dried out.

Was I getting *fired*? Usually, when they fired people, they called security in to watch them clean out their lockers while we all whispered about it in the hallway. Was this a precursor to the locker clean out?

My heart tripped in my chest when I walked into Caplan's office to see a tall, black-clad security guard standing in the center of the room. Bile rose in my throat. *Oh fuck, oh fuck.* This was it. I was getting fired today. For what? What had I done?

The guard turned as we entered, and my grip on reality started to slip.

"Asher?" I stared, my brain struggling to comprehend what I was seeing. The hot security guard from the gala was standing right there in front of Caplan's desk, arms crossed and looking grim.

"Hello, Miss Sanchez." He gave me a small smile that only curved up the corners of his mouth. "I wish we were meeting again under better circumstances."

"What?" It was the only thing that came to my mind as my heart thumped faster in my chest. I tried to slow my breathing. When had it gotten so fast? "You... you work for the hospital?"

"No, ma'am. I apologize, I know this must seem abrupt—"

"Am I being fired? Are you here to escort me out?" My head swiveled back and forth between Asher and Caplan.

My director winced, padding over to a pitcher of water on the sideboard. "Of course not, Rija. You're integral to our team. This is a matter of your personal security." He poured a glass and handed it to me with a bracing look. Like I was going to need something to hold on to for this conversation.

"Ma'am, perhaps you'd like to sit down? I can explain a few things before we head out."

"Head out?" The water in my cup rippled. I had a sudden, impeccably clear mental image of it slipping out of my hand and cracking open on the floor. I squeezed it tighter, holding it with two hands. "I still have to finish my shift. And then I have dinner at my parents' house…"

I trailed off. Asher was already shaking his head. "I'm afraid not, ma'am. We need to get you to a secure location ASAP."

"Secure…" I trailed off again, tired of just repeating everything he said. I took a breath and a sip of the water. It eased my dry throat enough that I started over. "I'm sorry. I don't understand what's happening."

Asher nodded gravely. "Yes, ma'am. I understand. Maybe you'd like to take a seat for this. I'm aware this might come as a shock." He waited for me to perch on one of the leather chairs facing Caplan's desk before he continued. "My company, RISI Securities, provides personal security services for Dr. Dobrev. Recently, he's received several threats to his life, and this morning, we received one targeting you—"

"Death threats?" I sprang to my feet, water sloshing around me. "Is Malachi alright?"

Asher reached his hand over, plucking the glass from my grasp and setting it lightly on the desk beside him. "Dr. Dobrev is fine. Safe at his apartment. I assure you, he is completely unharmed and will remain so for a very long time, if we have anything to say about it. Please."

He gestured again at my chair. Something about the soothing tone of his voice and the hint of his wry smile settled some of my nerves. Malachi was okay. That was good. But my head was still spinning. "He's been receiving death threats? How long has this been going on?"

Asher watched as I sank back onto the edge of the seat. I couldn't fully commit to the backrest right now, and he seemed fine with that. "Dr. Dobrev has had a stalker for some time. It seems his move to Chicago triggered something, and the threats began in earnest a few weeks ago. This morning, we received intelligence indicating that his aggressor is getting more serious, and is now focusing on you."

"I...but he's safe?" My palms weren't just sweating now, they were shaking. Hurting. I realized I'd clenched my fingers so hard there were little half-moon imprints in my skin.

"Yes, ma'am. Completely safe, I assure you. According to his personal protocols, once he is secure, our team has orders to likewise secure Sonia Dobrev, Joanne and Richard Dobrev, and you." That dry, unexpected smirk made an appearance. "I'm on Rija duty."

"I'm...on his security protocols?" Something about the concept overwhelmed me. I buried my face in my hands. Out of nowhere, a flood of tears prickled my eyes. I still didn't fully understand what was going on. All I knew was that Mal was in danger and had somehow still found a way to look out for me, even though he was miles away, across town in some sort of security lockdown.

My breath shuttered in and out, mind spinning to keep up. This was bad. Horribly, ridiculously bad, like something out of a movie. I pressed my hands harder against my face. *Focus, Rija.* I was trained in emergency response and triage. I could do better than this.

I bit my lip, the pain helping to center me. "How long has this been going on? The threats? The stalker?" I glanced up, hastily smearing tears away from my eyes. I could cry later, like maybe when I had Mal and Siggy in my arms and we were all a safe distance away from windows.

Asher nodded, his eyes warm and understanding. "That might be a conversation you have with Dr. Dobrev yourself. Would you like to speak to him? I've got strict orders to call him as soon as you're secure. Now that you've been briefed, we can exfiltrate."

"Yes, please, I'd like to talk to Malachi." My shoulders eased a centimeter at the thought. While Asher pulled out his phone, I glanced back at Caplan, who was still hovering by the water pitcher. My stomach lurched again. God, how must this look to him? I was a hard worker and always tried my best to conduct myself professionally. And now, suddenly, I was using his office as a refuge from my boyfriend's stalker? It was ridiculous.

"Director Caplan, I'm so sorry you're getting dragged into this." My fingers twisted in my lap. He shook his head, reaching over to give me a careful pat on the shoulder, like I could fall apart at any moment. I swiped my hands at the tears under my eyes again.

"Rija, really. Don't worry about a thing. Your safety is my priority here. Let us know what you need and we'll make it work, alright? Your job will still be here when all this has blown over. You understand me? That should not be your concern right now."

It hadn't been my concern until he'd said something about it. Double fuck. What would happen next? Tomorrow? This week? How long did it take to apprehend a stalker?

I didn't have any answers. Instead, I just gave Caplan a trembling smile, falling back on the etiquette my parents had drilled into me since before I could speak. *When in doubt, just smile and nod.* "Thank you, sir. That means a lot."

"Here you go. Answered on the first ring." Asher handed me a phone. I grabbed at it with both hands.

"Mal?"

"Rija! I'm so sorry. I swear, I thought we had it under control." His words rushed out of the speaker like they'd been bottled up for hours. The sound of his panicked voice sent a fresh wave of tears to my eyes. He sounded frantic.

"Are you okay? You're sure you're alright?"

His response was instant. "Yes, Ri. I'm absolutely fine. Are you?"

I glanced around, a surreal vertigo feeling ringing in my ears. "I'm not sure. I guess this all just feels so sudden and crazy. Mal, how long has this person been threatening you? Why didn't you tell me?"

He blew out a long breath. I could practically see him hunched over on the couch, scrubbing his hand down his face. "A long time, Kitten. Too long. I should have...done more for her. And now it's too late."

I sniffed, the regret in his voice not doing anything to help the tears that wouldn't stop running down my cheeks. "Her? Your stalker?"

"Yes, it's..." He paused, and I heard a low murmur in the background. "Rija, we'll have to talk about this when you're here. But you need to go." His words reached me right as Asher knelt down beside me.

"Miss Sanchez, we need to move out now. It's a lot easier to secure your apartment than it is to lock down the whole hospital." His warm green eyes didn't seem overly flustered or concerned, but his hand on my arm, urging me out of the chair, spurred me into action. I tried not to sway on numb feet when I stood.

"Right, I have to go. Crap, I don't have any of my stuff." Even as I spoke, Asher lifted my work bag from the floor at his feet, offering it to me. I took it automatically.

"We took the liberty of retrieving your things from your locker to speed things along."

His hand on my upper arm pushed me gently to the doorway while I stared down at the bag in my hand. I hadn't even noticed it sitting there. My other hand was still clutching Asher's phone to my ear, where I could hear Mal breathing softly. I shook my head to clear it.

"My locker was locked."

He fished in his pocket before pulling out the familiar hot pink combination lock. "No sweat." I blinked as he slid it into the outside pocket of my bag.

"O-okay. I—Director Caplan, I have to—"

Caplan nodded, waving me on. "We've already started calling people to handle your shifts this week. Be safe, Rija. We'll see you soon." He sounded more confident than I'd ever been in my entire life. I wanted to take comfort in his optimism, but I still felt like I was scrambling for a foothold.

It was a struggle to keep my legs and breath steady as Asher led me back down the hall. He murmured something into his earpiece. The same one I'd seen on my driver on my way to the gala. I sucked in a breath.

"Rija?" Mal asked in my ear, still on the line.

"All that security at the gala. That was for you? For this?" I remembered the security guards at the apartment that night, too. The ones I'd seen around the lobby over this past week. We used to only have one night guard. Why didn't I realize it before now?

In the two beats he paused before responding, my heart sank into my stomach. I knew his response before he even said anything. "Yes."

A burst of air left my throat. Like a sob or a cry or a shout. Maybe all of them put together. Asher's hand on my shoulder squeezed. "Why didn't you tell me, Mal? You've been dealing with this all by yourself? Has this...have all those 'work emergencies' really been about your stalker?"

"...Yes. I'm sorry, Kitten." My chest squeezed, more tears rolling. Just a few minutes ago, I'd been worried about my mother sniping at me, and for the last few weeks, Mal's life had been in danger? I could have lost him and never even known there was anything to be worried about.

"It's really not that big a deal," Mal assured me. "I received a threat that she'd try and get to me at the gala. It was quick work to put a screening team out front."

"Not a big deal?" I sobbed again, air trapped in my lungs. *I could have lost him.*

"It's their job, Ri. I know it seems like a lot. But I promise, everything is fine. This is...completely routine."

He was lying. I could tell he was. He was minimizing this situation and the danger he was in to make me feel better, to ease my struggling, sawing breaths.

I needed to get to him, right now, to see that he was alright with my own two eyes, and then shake him until whatever had come loose in his brain popped back into place.

Everything else seemed so insignificant now: My parents' disapproval, Sonia's reaction to our relationship...none of it mattered. Mal mattered. Sonia mattered. I needed to be with them, right now. We'd figure everything out, together.

"Where's Sonnie?" I asked, refusing to address his absurd claim that this was all routine. We'd discuss that later, in person, in private.

Asher ushered me through the door to the stairwell, pausing when I did. When I gave him a questioning look, he just pointed down.

"On her way to the airport. She's safe, I swear. She'll be here tonight."

"Okay. Okay," I repeated, eyeing the stairs, unsure if my shaky legs were up to the task. I turned back to Asher. "No elevator?"

"Exfiltrate," he nodded with a smirk. "We're going to be a bit sneaky."

"Okay." I started down. "I'm coming, Mal."

"Yes, good, just get here and we'll talk. We'll figure everything else out, Ri, I swear."

I gulped, gripping the phone so tightly I could feel the ridges of the case on my finger pads. Next to me, Asher eased the duffel bag out of my hand and tossed it over his shoulder. I hadn't even noticed I'd been struggling with it. Now that it was gone, I realized it had been heavy. Had they emptied my whole locker in there?

I had too many questions and hardly any answers. Just stairs. Ten floors' worth of them.

"Mal, will you stay with me? While I get there?"

"Always, Love. Always."

Chapter 11

A soft knock sounded at the door. "Dr. Dobrev? Miss Sanchez? Miss Dobrev is coming up now."

Mal stirred underneath me. I was curled up on top of him on our bed. Air pressed around us, warm and stuffy. The RISI team had sealed the apartment and was methodically checking every possible entry point. The trash chute had been unsealed ("Too steep to be a threat," Asher had assured us.), but they were still checking the vents, so we'd been stewing all afternoon without any air conditioning.

The inside of the apartment was eerily quiet, except for Siggy's snores, the soft movements of our security guard in the living room, and Mal's shallow breathing. We hadn't spoken a word to each other in hours, not since I'd come home and he'd spilled the whole story to me.

"Malachi. Cariño," I'd whispered. His arms had enveloped me the second the elevator doors opened. He'd held me tight enough that I'd had a hard time taking in a full breath of air. A shame, since now I was with him, I felt like I could finally breathe again. He hadn't let me go since.

"What time is it?" I murmured now, rolling to a seat as Siggy stretched to follow. Time had taken on an odd sort of flow. Hours passed by in a blink, but it seemed like we'd already been here for days. All the curtains were drawn. In rooms where we hadn't hung them yet, Asher and our other guard from RISI, Grayson, used sheets and moving blankets to block the windows.

"Interrupts lines of sight from below. For shooters." I'd shivered at Asher's explanation. That was when Mal had taken me back to the bedroom for some privacy. We hadn't slept, hadn't turned the TV on. Just laid here, Siggy nestled at the small of my back.

Mal's phone flashed in the dark. "After midnight."

I yawned as I made my way to the hallway. I was exhausted, unable to sleep. Not while Sonia was still out there, dealing with a flight delay as she made her way home. I had a sneaking suspicion that even when she got here, I still wouldn't be able to shut down completely. I was too wired. On edge, despite the many assurances I got from the RISI team that they had everything under control. I believed them, but everything still felt out of control and surreal.

Asher and Grayson, who was a few years older and seemed to be in charge, were in and out of the apartment constantly, rotating between securing the apartment building and doing something on computers in our living room. They both had guns clipped to their belts and the coiling wires of earpieces snaking out of the collars of their black shirts.

I really was living in a movie.

Siggy and Mal padded behind me. I picked up my pace when I heard the elevator doors open with a *ding*.

"Sonnie?" I yelled, my feet skidding on the wooden floors when I took the hallway corner too fast. Mal was right on my tail.

"Rija? Malachi?"

I clutched my chest when I heard her voice, barreling past Asher and careening straight into my best friend, all but ignoring Grayson, who had taken one of the RISI Rovers to pick Sonnie up from the airport.

I was sobbing before we'd even closed our arms around each other. We all rocked, tipping precariously when Malachi slammed into my back, gathering us both up against him.

We laughed and sniffled and shuffled to stay upright, clinging to each other like one of us would die if we let go.

"Sonnie, I'm so sorry." Mal had apologized so much tonight that I'd barred him from saying it again to me. Sonia was equally disinclined to put up with his bullshit.

"Mal, it's not your fault that some psycho is stalking you." Her voice wavered in a way I'd only ever heard a few times. I hugged her closer. I couldn't stand to hear my usually bubbly, irreverent friend so close to tears. She continued, voice strained. "If anything, it's my fault—"

"It's not. You can't..." Mal squeezed us tighter. "We can't blame ourselves."

"Deal." Sonnie pulled back, palming both our cheeks and looking at us like we'd been apart for years, not just two weeks. Her face collapsed, and I saw the first tear fall just before she yanked us back into the group hug. "I'm so glad you're both alright."

"We're fine. We're all safe. Grayson and Asher will make sure of that."

"Yes. Right." Sonia pulled away, swiping at the mascara from under her eyes. I wanted to pull her back, but she was already stepping toward the two men where they stood huddled together, giving each other hushed updates. They broke off when Sonia approached.

"You're Asher?" she demanded.

"Yes, ma'am." Asher stepped forward. Sonia kept walking closer, studying him.

"You really are as hot as you sound on the phone." Her voice shook even as she made the joke. Asher's mouth twisted into that wry grin.

"Back atcha, ma'am."

"Don't call me ma'am." Her command lost its power since she sighed it and simultaneously launched herself into his arms. He caught her around the waist, brows pulling down in confusion when she pulled him into the same sort of full-body, full-drama hug we'd just had with her.

"Thank you for keeping my family safe," she whispered. His face softened as he swallowed, making gentle circles around her shoulder blades.

"Of course, ma—" he caught himself. "Miss Dobrev. It's my job."

She hummed. We all watched as the hug drew out for another second. Two. Three...Four. Asher's eyes flicked to Grayson. The other man's eyes narrowed, pointedly staring at where Asher's hands rested on Sonnie's back. Asher coughed and lifted his arms.

"Er, this seems gratuitous." He gave her a cautious pat between her shoulder blades.

"It is," Sonnie sighed. Her arm moved lower. Asher's eyes widened in shock just before she pulled away.

"Sonnie," I couldn't help the watery laugh that stuttered out of me. "You can't feel up the security team." Even as I admonished, I pulled her into another hug. I'd missed her and today had been horrible and sometimes a girl just needed her best friend.

"Not both of them. Just that one, and I have no regrets." At her words, another strangled cough escaped my formerly unflappable bodyguard. The smile she gave me was half-hearted at best, tinged with sadness when she looked at her brother. "You should have told me, Mal."

"I know." He shook his head, face a mixture of regret and grief I'd become familiar with in the last few hours. "I know."

"Come on," I pulled both him and Sonnie down the hallway to the living room. We didn't need to have this conversation standing around in front of the elevator.

"I had a right to know. She was my friend." Sonnie's words struck home, and Malachi winced as they sat on the couch, Mal on one side, and Sonia in the corner of the sectional. My fearless, feisty friend pulled her legs up to her chest. She looked small.

I squeezed his hand before retreating to the kitchen to open a bottle of wine. He'd already explained the whole situation to me, and I had a feeling Sonia would take it even more poorly than I did. Maybe it was best to give them some space.

If I wracked my brain, I could remember her mentioning Christine, her freshman year roommate who'd had such a big crush on Malachi that she'd followed them to dinner one night. Apparently, the stalking hadn't ended there. It hadn't ended at all. She'd become obsessed with him, upending her life to follow him—stalk him—to Colorado, despite him telling her time and time again that he wasn't interested.

"I thought we had it under control. She was in treatment at an amazing program in Boulder. I just...I should have worked harder to make sure her doctor was handling this." Malachi sighed. I could hear the guilt in his voice, and I hated it for many reasons. So did Sonnie.

"Managing the mental health of *your stalker* is not your responsibility," she snapped, leaning forward to grip his shoulders and shake him the way I'd wanted to earlier today. "She's been following you around and threatening you for years. You should have let the police handle it. Tell him, Ri!" She twisted around to glare at me.

I removed the cork with a *pop*. "Trust me, I've already told him." The entire story had come spilling out as soon as I'd gotten home from the hospital earlier today. I was still emotionally spinning between fear and anger. Love. Because while Malachi had filed a restraining order against Christine, he'd simultaneously worked with a mental health facility in Colorado to get her the help she needed, and had employed private security to deal with her threats instead of the police. When I'd demanded to know why he hadn't worked harder to take legal action and lock her up, he'd looked at me, eyes shining with passion and empathy.

"She's unwell, Ri. My job is to help people. What else was I supposed to do?"

Even now, thinking about his earnest response broke my heart. Leave it to Dr. Do-Right to try and save everyone—including his stalker.

"Well, it ends now. It's not just me she's coming after, anymore." Mal swallowed, grimly accepting the glass of wine I handed him.

I tried not to imagine the crumpled letter Grayson had grudgingly slid across the counter earlier today. None of the men had wanted me to see it, but I felt I had a right, especially after they'd showed me a few of her more recent threats against Mal. Emails, handwritten cards, and sloppy scribbles, wildly ranging from professing her deep, undying love for him, and explaining in excruciating detail how she was going to harm him. I thought I'd hit some sort of numb threshold of horror, until they finally handed over the newest communication.

The grainy, enlarged photo of Mal and I, leaving the Gala hand-in-hand was marred, mutilated by dark, dripping ink that I didn't want to examine too closely. The words "She's dead" scrawled across my face.

I had shoved the picture back into Grayson's hands. Quickly.

Christine had gone ballistic when word got out that Mal was moving to Chicago to open up a new clinic. When he'd received her threat to show up at the gala, where he'd been publicized as the keynote speaker, Mal had immediately called her doctor in Colorado. By the time they'd gotten someone to her apartment, she'd been long gone, on her way here.

Asher and Grayson had been working all week since the gala, discretely shadowing Mal to work, while splitting their time coordinating with our building's security and trying to find her. But there was a lot of ground to cover between Boulder and Chicago, and looking for a single woman who didn't want to be found was like trying to find a needle in a haystack.

It wasn't until this morning, and the bloody handwriting scribbled across my image, that Mal had reached his limit. The RISI team had handed over all their investigation material to the police and locked Mal down. Their sole focus was now only on babysitting us until Christine was caught.

The mentally unwell woman who wanted to kill us.

Another chill rattled my spine, even in the stuffy, warm air of the penthouse.

I'd changed into one of Mal's old sweatshirts, leggings, and a pair of fuzzy socks when I'd come home, and I still shivered every once in a while. Mal grabbed my hand as I sat next to him, tangling our fingers together.

"She'll go to jail after this. I'm not fucking around with your safety," he assured me, thumb sweeping across my knuckles. His declaration made me melt while simultaneously spiking my furious, protective anger.

"But you're fine with her threatening *you?*" I demanded, not for the first time today. I couldn't imagine living my life with a stalker out in the world, and just going about my day.

Mal rubbed his forehead, squeezing my hand. "We had it under control. She was doing well...I hadn't gotten a letter or anything from her in *years*. She was living on her own. I thought it was fine. I'm sorry."

I shook my head at his apology. He'd made his decisions, and I knew he'd probably still help her if he had the chance again. "I just wish you'd have taken threats against your life as seriously as you took them against mine."

His lips brushing against my wrist was the only response I got. The grim determination in his eyes was answer enough. He felt perfectly fine taking risks with his own life, but he'd stop at nothing to protect me. Infuriating. And so damn sweet. That look knocked the breath out of my lungs.

It was love. Fierce and true. Even in the face of all the chaos and sadness of the day, my heart swelled. I'd known he was attracted to me. Liked me. Assumed that maybe he even was on his way to loving me, but all my assumptions were obliterated in the face of the stark reality.

This man loved me as much as I loved him. In a big, sweeping, *this is it* kind of way. He'd upended his world for me—not just to give us a chance at a relationship, but to give us a chance to start our lives together. I swallowed back tears, reaching over to grip his forearm.

"They're very close. Great friends." Sonia's voice broke the spell that had fallen over me and Mal. I blinked, my gaze darting back to where she was staring at my hands. *Crap.* I'd known we'd have to tell Sonia that we were together, but the thought had taken a backseat to everything else going on today.

But now she was *here*, in Mal's apartment, which was also pretty much mine. My brain stuttered as I tried to remember the speech I'd prepared two weeks ago.

It seemed like a lifetime had passed since then.

"Sonnie, we—"

"Of course, I'm her *best* friend and she never looked at me like that. Like she wants to have my babies." Sonia craned her head, addressing Grayson as he walked through the room. "When's the last time you planted a desperate kiss on a pal's hand, huh? Looked soulfully into their eyes like your next breath depended on it?"

The man in question smirked but didn't respond. As he made his way to the office where the security team had set up their temporary headquarters, his bright, moss-green eyes danced in our direction. They saw right through us.

Apparently, so did Sonia.

Mal shifted, setting his wine down on the coffee table. I did the same, leaning forward to brace my arms on my legs.

I took a breath. "Sonnie—"

"For fuck's sake, cut the drama! Are you together or not? Because I swear to God, I have been gone for two weeks and if you two haven't gotten with the program, I will lock you in a room and blast Marvin Gaye through the door, if I have to." She eyed us, exasperated, as she took a sip of her wine.

My mouth dropped open. "You...?" I gasped at the same time Malachi's incredulous "What?" echoed through the room. Sonia rolled her eyes.

"Guys, I'm flighty. Not stupid. You two have been making gross sexy eyes at each other for months. *Years*, even. I'd have to be completely blind and on another planet not to see it." She took another sip before putting her glass down on the table with ours.

"But you said I had to stay away. Keep my hands off?"

Sonnie scoffed, leaning forward to place her hands over our tightly clenched fingers. "It is amazing and stupid that you took something I said years ago so seriously. It's been obvious over these last few months that you were falling for him. I brought it up again as, like, a joke. I kept waiting for you to tell me, Ri. Both of you." Her attention flickered to Mal before landing back on my face. "When you didn't, I figured I was standing in the way. I tried to tell you right before I left, but shit-for-brains over here interrupted us."

She flicked Mal's arm affectionately. He grumbled and brushed her off, but she continued. "Rija, I know you're not going anywhere. You're like a sister to me. Now, I see there's enough of you for both of us. I just want you to be happy. *Both of you*." She repeated, flicking Mal again, this time on his earlobe.

"*That's* why you left so suddenly for New York?" he demanded, batting her hand away from his head. Sonia threw her hands in the air.

"Yes, my God, I practically told you two to maul each other, hoping to break the seal. Please tell me it worked because I've got to come back home eventually and Jesus Christ, the *pining* you two have been doing is giving me an ulcer."

"Sonia..." I trailed off, shaking my head in disbelief. I'd been worried for so long about her reaction to me and Mal's relationship, and here she was actively trying to throw us together?

I felt like I'd been held up by strings, the tension pulling me taught, and all at once, they'd been snipped. I was strangely loose. Tired and floppy. Like I could breathe for the first time in six months. My head fell forward. "Why didn't you say anything? I've been freaking out."

"Why didn't *you* say anything?" She huffed as I felt Mal's warm fingers massaging the back of my neck. "I thought you weren't sure yet, or something? I'm not trying to pimp my brother out unless it's for true love, you know? So?" She had the audacity to sound like *we* were the frustrating ones. "Are you together or not? Because I will get creative if I need to."

I raised my head, eyes landing on Mal, who shook his head. Brown eyes danced with laughter.

"Yes, we're together," he murmured. A softer version of that fierce, raw affection from earlier took over his face.

"Yeah, I...kind of live here now." A disbelieving breath huffed out of me. Because it was true, and I was telling Sonnie and she didn't look mad or disappointed. Her lips softened into a quiet smile. Her hands reached towards mine, and our fingers grasped. Best friends. Thicker than thieves. Sisters.

"And you're happy?" she whispered, as if it were even a question.

"Yes," I whispered back. I glanced up at Mal when he eased a few strands of hair out of my face.

"Very," he agreed, grinning down at me. "Present circumstances excluded, of course."

"Aw, you guyssss!"

Mal and I rocked backwards as Sonnie threw herself at us, looping her arms around our necks in a clumsy group hug. "I'm just happy you're happy. Three musketeers!"

She squeezed me hard enough to make me cough. A strangled wheeze from Mal told me he was receiving the same treatment. I reached up to pat her back, feeling Mal's arm creep around me until we were all tangled up together. My two best friends, and not a single secret between us.

"This is nice, but at some point we're going to have to talk about Sonnie's questionable taste in smash music. Marvin Gaye? You need to modernize." Mal thumped his sister on the back. She reluctantly let go of us, standing to swig the rest of her wine. I saw her swipe a finger under her eye. She wasn't the only one feeling misty.

All at once, the pressure of the day and the guilt and regrets of the last six months caught up to me and I slumped back into the cushions. My head felt fuzzy, eyes already drooping. We were all safe, with two big, burly security men standing between us and the danger. Mal and I were together, and Sonnie was happy about it. I felt like I could give myself permission to pass out.

"Don't be judgy. Dare I even ask what's on your playlist?" She glared at him.

"Gotta be Boyz II Men," he grinned, his hand reaching back to squeeze my thigh. I gave him a sleepy smile.

"Gag. What about you, Hot Asher? What's on your smash list?"

"I won't lie. It's a lot of Beyoncé," Asher answered without looking up from his computer. A faint smirk played on his lips. Sonia had been heading towards the kitchen with her wine glass, but his response made her stop in her tracks. She studied him for a beat before he looked up to meet her eyes. His smirk deepened.

"Surprising and intriguing choice, Hot Asher." She looked him up and down. I could practically see her cataloging his features. The tattoos peeking out from his sleeve, the tousled brown hair, and his teasing expression. She bit her lip, and his gaze followed the movement. "I was going to ask where my bedroom was, but I think I should ask where yours is instead."

"You'll be in the guest room next to the primary suite, where Agent Kaine can monitor you. From the hallway," Grayson intoned from the across the room as he exited the study. Asher snapped his attention back to the computer screen in front of him. I couldn't tell in the low lights of the room, but I thought I saw a blush creep across his cheekbones.

"Sonnie, try not to get our security staff fired on the first day of a crisis," Mal chided, leaning back to look into my eyes. "You look tired, Kitten."

"Everything's going to be alright, Mal. Sonia's here...everything will be okay."

He pressed a soft kiss to my nose. "Yes, it will. I'll make sure of it. Come on, you're barely keeping your eyes open."

"I can walk," I protested when strong arms scoop me against his hard chest.

"Of course you can, but why?"

I mumbled a goodnight to Sonia, who was quietly trying to charm Grayson. She probably felt bad about distracting his team. Mal pressed another kiss to my forehead as I snuggled into his chest. I was asleep before he laid me on the bed.

Chapter 12

"She's just trying to draw you out. Get a rise out of you," Asher warned in a hard voice. Next to me, Mal's knuckles were turning white where his fingers clenched around his coffee mug.

"I'm aware," he gritted. I reached over to push his hand down, forcing him to set the mug on the table in front of him. Any more tension and we'd have shattered ceramic and a tepid macchiato all over our breakfast table. His fingers flexed as he watched the words scroll across the screen.

Dr. Do-Right Did Me Wrong!

Last night, Christine had uploaded the weepy, confessional-style video to social media, tagging all the major gossip sites. Adam was beside himself.

On the screen, teary-eyed and twisting her fingers, a brunette woman spewed an utterly fabricated story on a grainy cell-phone video.

"...loved him so much. But when I told him about the baby, he lost his mind. I...I still can't believe the things he said." Christine sobbed into the camera, dabbing at her eyes. "The stress of it all...I lost the baby. And he didn't even care. Now, I see him in Chicago with these other women. I just don't want what happened to me to happen to someone else."

"Dr. Dobrev, known by his social media handle, 'Dr. Do-Right' has in fact been spotted with at least two women in Chicago, where he is opening a new clinic," the anchor on the entertainment news show droned while pictures flicked across the screen: Mal and Sonia walking out of our apartment complex a few weeks ago, images of him and I at the gala, hanging all over each other. "Eyewitness reports say Dr. Dobrev was definitely getting cozy with at least one of them."

"I mean, I hear a lot of stuff while I'm driving people around, but he was talking about taking her back home and getting her clothes off. I'm not sure what he was saying is appropriate for TV, you know? It was pretty graphic."

I gasped, jerking forward to get a closer look at the TV. "You're shitting me! Isn't that our driver from the gala?"

The man on the screen turned. Once I got a look at his profile and the same black baseball hat as he'd had on that night, I knew it was. Asher tensed as he watched the man detail his interactions with us that night, including how Mal had handed over a wad of cash and asked him to keep what he'd heard quiet. Mal cursed, head dropping into his hands.

"That's one of the contractors we used for transport on the sixteenth," Grayson muttered. He was an intimidating guy, but now the flat, no-nonsense voice I'd become accustomed to held an icy edge that made me want to shrink away, slowly. "Track him down."

"Already on it," Asher bit out, hammering on his laptop keyboard.

"Call Callihan, too," Grayson added.

"We're on a secure chat now," Asher nodded. "Boss says cut ties with the contracting company and make that asshole wish he'd never learned to speak."

"Then let's make it so," Grayson commanded. Asher was already bringing his phone up to his ear. A perfectly oiled machine.

Sonia gave me a *what the fuck look* before turning her head to watch Asher pace behind the couch. I wasn't sure what it meant to make a guy wish he'd never learned to speak, but I didn't want to ask too many questions.

Grayson had been gone most of the morning, personally running surveillance around the building and doing whatever needed to be done outside the apartment. Asher, it seemed, was going to stay with us. He'd parked himself in the far corner of the room where he could see everyone and spent the last few hours typing a lot and talking to someone named Dex about tapping surveillance feeds.

It seemed like a lot of action, but they both had that same steady, confident presence Asher had shown when he'd picked me up at the hospital. They went out of their way to explain what they were doing, giving us updates and working to make us feel comfortable in the least comfortable situation known to man.

I liked them. Over the last twenty-four hours, I'd felt safe with them. Getting this peek into the more ruthless side of their business was chilling.

"Did you really try to bribe that guy to forget he heard you talk about…" I trailed off, fairly certain that Sonnie wouldn't want to hear about Mal's plans to bend me over the couch.

"I promise I was just trying to protect your virtue." Mal sighed, still staring at the TV. "Though, I'll admit, it sounds pretty sinister in this context."

The entertainment reporters had moved on to some other story about an heiress and her recent divorce, but I could see him reliving the footage again and again in his brain. I cupped his neck, turning him to look at me.

"Hey. It'll be okay." I'd repeated it so many times it was practically a mantra this morning. "It's like Asher said. She's just trying to get a rise out of you so she can get to us. All this will die down soon and we'll just go back to our lives. Walking Siggy and threatening to throw the espresso machine off the balcony."

His smile didn't reach his tired eyes. "For the record, I've never threatened to throw the espresso machine off the balcony."

"Well, don't be surprised if it's missing one day. Soon. Once we can open the patio doors again, it's game over for that thing." I knew I was being ridiculous, but it was the only thing I could think of to wipe that pained, broody look off his face.

His hand reached for mine. His expression softened into something calmer. Fond. "Rija, I—" His phone vibrated on the table between us, Adam's face popping up on the screen. Mal sighed. "I have to get this. He could be having an aneurysm or something."

I watched Mal walk away to answer the call and make another coffee. Despite all the excitement from yesterday and my dragging exhaustion, both of us had woken up before the dawn, when we'd felt the air conditioning kick back on. Asher assured us they'd mounted motion sensors throughout the ducts, so it was safe to open the vents again.

Even with his reassurance, I hadn't been able to fall back asleep. Sonnie had joined us as soon as she'd heard the coffee machine running, so we'd all had a front-row seat to the first news clip of Christine and her lies dropping on E News.

"This makes me want to throw *her* off the balcony," Sonia seethed into her espresso. Her nose wrinkled in a way I recognized. She was getting emotional and trying not to be. "I can't believe she was my friend once. I mean, she's so...I couldn't imagine doing something like...."

"Don't beat yourself up." It was Asher, not me, who offered the advice, even though almost the same words had been on the tip of my tongue. He paused on his way back to his post in the corner, flipping his phone around and around in his hands. "Of course you couldn't imagine someone doing this. She has severe behavioral health issues and you..." His eyes flicked over Sonnie, lingering on her short cotton sleep shorts. "You don't know what that's like. *Do* you?" His mouth twisted in a smirk, teasing.

I had to applaud his attempt at distracting her. Especially when it worked.

"I've been told my whole dominatrix thing is more of a hobby than a diagnosis."

Asher's smirk vanished, eyes sharpening. "That didn't come up in our background check."

"I'm happy to give you a one-on-one interview, if the information is necessary."

"Critical," he glowered. My eyes ping-ponged between the two of them. Sonia was as much of a dominatrix as Siggy was, but apparently the truth didn't matter when she was trying to seduce our personal security.

I would have said their flirting was weird, since it was happening right in the middle of a major crisis, but after he walked away and Sonnie's gaze followed him, I couldn't help but notice the tense set of her shoulders had relaxed just a smidge. When she bit into the bagel Asher had conveniently left at the table, right in front of her, I wondered if Asher was really into the flirting, or if he was just really good at knowing how to put my friend at ease. Or both.

"Maleficent alert," Sonia warned, glaring at my phone. My mother's name scrolled silently across the top.

I cursed, swiping the device off the table to glare at the screen. I'd called my mom last night to briefly tell her we weren't going to make it to dinner because of the active threats. As expected, she'd had more questions about the dinner than the stalker. She'd texted and called so many times last night, no doubt hoping she could bully us into reconsidering our attendance, that I'd flipped my phone to silent.

Her name vanished from my screen, the phone helpfully informing me of the *Missed call from Rosalia Sanchez*. I only saw the words for a second before her name popped up again. I cursed again.

"Here, give it to me. I'll tell her to fuck off."

I yanked the phone away before Sonia could grab it, knowing she was dead serious about following through.

"I'm just going to answer. I don't want to dodge her calls all day." I tapped on the screen, bringing the phone to my ear, ignoring Sonia's huffy sigh. "Hi, Mom."

"Marija! Are you seeing these accusations about that man? It's all over the news!"

I rolled my eyes. So far, we'd seen more traction on social media than the news. Christine's story was only playing on entertainment channels and a few of the gossipier morning shows. I caught Sonnie's gaze, watching as she threateningly took a breath, like she was about to shout a massive *fuck you* into my phone's speaker. I popped up from my chair, high-tailing it to my bedroom before she could properly fill her lungs.

"Mama, that woman is the stalker I told you about. Obviously, Malachi didn't get her pregnant, then leave her."

"And there are pictures of you in that God-awful red dress, too," my mother rambled on without acknowledging my comment. "I've already gotten three calls about it, Marija. One from Melissa Peterson."

"Oh, God, not Melissa Peterson!" I wasn't sure if it was the lack of sleep, excess caffeine coursing through me, or the overall stress of everything going on, but the sarcastic exclamation popped out of me before I could regulate it. My mother's answering hiss was enough to make me flop backwards onto the bed, covering my eyes with my forearm.

"I don't know what makes you think this is funny, young lady—"

"It's not funny," I cut her off. I'd never spoken to my mother like this before, but in for a penny, in for a pound and all that. It was always easier to handle my mom over the phone, when I didn't have to deal with her intimidating glares and blanket disapproval.

Right now, laying on the bed I shared with Malachi, knowing my best friend was safe in the next room and there was a stalker out there trying to fuck us all up, I didn't want to deal with her *at all*. "Maybe you thought I was joking last night, but I'll reiterate that there is a stalker out there making threats against my life, and Mal's. Forgive me if I'm more concerned with that than a thirty-second news clip."

"And I'll repeat what *I* said last night, that these celebrity types always have someone coming after them. Who's to say she's not telling the truth?" At her casual accusation, I hissed in my own breath, but she raised her voice when I tried to correct her. "All I know is that *my daughter* has been traipsing around with that vulgar man, and it's unacceptable."

"That man—"

"He and his sister both have been nothing but trouble the second you met them. Before that girl showed up, you were on the right track—"

"I *never* wanted to be a doctor. How many times do I have to tell you that?"

"—and now her brother is dragging you into some scandal. Enough is enough, Marija!"

"You're right, Mom." My arm slid off my face and I rubbed at my eyes. I was running low on sleep and energy and fucks to give. I felt like I'd hit some sort of emotional rock bottom, where I had nothing left. Listening to my mother disparage my favorite people in the world, my *true family*, had sucked me dry.

"Well, thank the Lord you're seeing some sense now. Your father and I will find you a new apartment. You simply can't be around those people anymore—"

"No. *No, Mom*," I snapped louder when she didn't stop talking. One benefit of being my mother's daughter: I'd learned her tricks. The scathing authority in my voice made even the great Rosalia Sanchez pause. It should have felt good or vindicating, finally, to get her attention. I just felt tired.

"I meant, enough is enough with you." I swallowed, rushing on before she could stop me. "I already got a new apartment. With Malachi. He's not going anywhere, Mom. And Sonnie is more family to me than our actual family is. She's not going anywhere, either."

"I...wh....you..." I'd never heard my mother literally sputter before. Somewhere in the back of my brain, a small part of me was cheering. Most of me, though, just felt a little sad.

I wished things could have been different. I wished my parents could just see me for me, and not what they wanted me to be. That they didn't only pay attention to me when it suited their needs or reputation. I wished I got half the support from them that I did from Sonia and Mal.

But wishes weren't reality. "I fail to see how *that girl* can be more family to you than I am."

"*That girl* held me when I cried for days when *you* practically disowned me just because I didn't go to med school. And *that vulgar man* is the man I love. He's my future, and I won't allow you to drag him through the mud just because of some stupid news story." I wasn't sure how my voice could sound so strong when my pulse was going haywire. Even my breathing felt uneven, but this conversation was long overdue. I wouldn't stop now.

"You have to be—"

"I understand this may be upsetting to you, but I'm done with constantly being burdened by your disappointments. Those are your failures, not mine. I won't let you pin them on me or the people I love."

Listening to her shocked inhale, I could envision her red face, veins bulging, probably perched on her favorite chaise in the sitting room.

When I was in therapy last year, Dr. Peterson told me if I ever wanted to set a boundary with my parents, I should be prepared for them to push back. For them to be defensive and pile blame at my feet.

Back then, even thinking about having this conversation had put a black pit in my stomach. Now, though, when my life was literally being threatened and I still couldn't catch a break, I was ready for it.

The thought of living a life without having to nod and smile and show up at some fundraiser just because my parents told me to was freeing. Never having to go to another brutal family get-together, watching them fawn over my cousins just because they had a more advanced medical degree than I did? Bliss.

I was done with all that. With them. More than done.

"I will not allow my own daughter to speak to me like this."

"That's fine. It's probably best if we let some time pass before we speak again." I took a deep breath, trying to ease the tightness in my chest.

I'd practiced many, many times what I'd say to my parents when I finally confronted them. I had versions where I was crying, where *they* were crying, where we were angry or sad or quietly accepting of each other. Right now, I liked the calm, convicted version.

"When you're ready to talk again without belittling me and the people I love, I'd be open to discussing ways we can still have a relationship. You, me, and Dad, if he's willing. But I'm done with this now. I'm not interested in being your daughter, if it means feeling like shit every time we speak to each other."

"Marija Sanchez!" She was gearing up for the mother of all lectures. I could feel it. I stared up at the ceiling. The fan spun lazily, doing nothing to cool my heated skin.

"Mom, aren't you tired?" I whispered, willing my voice to stay steady, just for a little longer. Just until this was over and I could process it without her seething on the other end of the phone. "Because I'm so tired. I've never been the person you wanted me to be, and it's taken its toll."

"Marija..." She sighed, her voice softening by a degree. I blinked away the tears forming at the corners of my eyes. I was going to be strong, dammit. I needed space and she needed to hear this.

"It hurts so much. Every time you say something about my clothes or my job or my friends. I can't even get a haircut without you commenting on it. Like the whole reputation of this family rests on the state of my split ends. It's exhausting. And I'm not doing it anymore. Especially when you drag the people I love into this. I've taken so much from you and dad for so long, but I draw the line at them.

"Sonia and Malachi are good people. The best people. And there isn't just someone 'gunning for him,' Mom. There is a person who is trying to kill us. Right now. You haven't once asked me if I'm alright, or offered to come see me or help or do *anything*."

"I...well, I'm sure the security people have it well in hand..."

"They do. Because Malachi made sure of it. He's made sure I was okay. And he managed to do it without insulting every aspect of my life." Alright, well, that sounded a little bitter. Maybe my calm approach had reached its limit. The anger of years and years of quiet, snide little cuts was bubbling to the surface.

"Mija, we only want what's best for you," she started. I interrupted again. Damn, if only past Rija could see me now. I never would have believed it. Then again, there were a lot of things happening right now I was still having trouble wrapping my mind around.

"What's best is that I'm happy. I've never understood why you were so against me just...being happy..." A choked breath hitched in my throat. Hot tears rolled down my temples. The fan spun slowly on.

"Marija..." I didn't even recognize Mom's voice now. She had never sounded so quiet or unsure. Not that I could remember. It didn't matter. I'd said my piece, and she'd either respect it or she wouldn't.

"Like I said, I think we should take some time before speaking again. Tell Dad, too. If you're ready to speak to me without tearing me down, we'll talk."

"Marija! Wait, just, could you please....text us with updates about the...stalker?" She whispered the last, like she couldn't bear to say the word out loud. "I suppose I didn't realize how serious it was."

My heart wrenched. I wasn't sure if that was a good idea, or if going completely no contact was best right now. I had a lot going on and they'd made my life miserable for so long and...and they were still my family. What if this was the wake-up call they'd needed? We *all* had needed?

I sighed. No matter how strong or mean or spiteful I wanted to be, I figured there would always be a small part of me that still wanted their approval. Still wanted *them*.

I was going to have to call Dr. Peterson again soon.

"I'll let you know when I'm safe. Goodbye, Mom." I hung up before she could get another word in edgewise. I dropped my phone somewhere to the right of my head, expecting it to erupt in angry vibrations as my mother called back.

It was silent on the white cotton duvet. More tears leaked into my hairline.

"I know it's only nine a.m., but is it too early to go back to bed?"

My head jerked up at the sound of Mal's voice. He was standing against the closed door to our room, looking at me with velvet soft eyes. My heart sank.

Chapter 13

"How much of that did you hear?" I croaked, sitting up and swiping at my face. I frantically replayed the conversation with my mother in my head. I'd said a lot of things, but what, specifically, had I said about Mal?

That I'd moved in with him. That I loved him. He was my future. *Ah, fuck.* I wanted to tell him those things myself, at the right time. Not when there was a crazy stalker on the loose trying to ruin his career. Not because he'd overheard me talking to my mother, of all people.

"Enough to be completely awed by you," he answered, already padding across the floor towards me. "You were so strong, Ri, standing up to her like that. I've never been more proud of you."

One second I was sitting on the duvet, the next, my ass was planted in his lap while he held me in the most tender embrace I'd ever felt. My eyes prickled again, but for a different reason.

"You're proud of me?" I squeaked. Malachi's hand swept across my face, coming away wet with my tears. He dropped kisses across my other cheek. The way he was holding me made me want to stay here forever.

"So proud. Ridiculously proud. It's hard to set boundaries like that with close family, but I knew you could do it, Ri. I knew it." He nuzzled the side of my neck. My eyes closed, and I curled myself deeper into him. I hadn't stopped crying yet, and my heart was still hammering in my ears. Run-ins with my mother always left me shaky, but this was helping. A lot.

"Apparently, I just needed the right motivation to cut her loose."

It wasn't the first time we'd talked about this, he and I. It was Mal's occupational hazard: getting up close and personal with someone else's life shit. Talking to them about it. Asking questions. Digging deeper.

Every time we talked about my parents, he always told me the same things. That I was worthy of love, especially from the people who were supposed to love me most. That I was allowed to make my own choices about my life. And that whatever I decided to do about my parents, whenever I decided to do it, he'd be with me all the way.

Looking back, this conversation, this breaking point, was inevitable. Maybe he and Dr. Peterson had always known that would be the case.

"Death threats have a way of offering some perspective, I suppose," he murmured, rocking me slightly against him. His fingers threaded through my hair.

"That, yes," I admitted. "And she was talking about how you and Sonnie are bad influences on me and had never been any good. I couldn't let her talk about you like that."

Mal stilled his stroking, craning down to look at my face. His brow furrowed softly, like he was asking a question, or he'd misheard me. "You cut your parents off because of me?"

"And Sonnie," I qualified, not sure why I felt the need to do so. I also wasn't sure why my eyes darted away to stare at the framed Jackson Pollock print across the room that we'd yet to hang. "Besides, she was saying stuff like maybe Christine was telling the truth, and I kind of cracked."

"Hmm." Mal breathed out a deep, growly sigh. "You know her whole story, the baby and everything, is a lie."

I jerked upright. Since we'd seen the video this morning, and the subsequent social media commentary, we hadn't discussed Christine's story. I'd assumed we didn't have to.

"Of course it's a lie, Mal. You would never do that to someone. You'd stand by your child, if you had one. Even if you had one with someone who is completely disturbed." My fingers wrapped around his chin when he continued to study the swirling pattern on my yoga pants. "I know you better than that. I know that what she's saying...it isn't possible. Not for you."

He took a quiet breath, let it out slowly.

"Rija, I've never had sex with Christine. Not even when we first met. But even if I had, she wouldn't be pregnant with my child. She couldn't." His black-brown irises bored into mine.

"You can't have kids?" That seemed like what he was trying to tell me, but I wanted to make sure I was reading it right. He looked so serious, so concerned. I knew this was important to him. Which made it important to me.

"I can't. She's not the first to threaten to make such...claims about me. Years ago, after all the social media stuff started taking off, before I'd met you, I had a vasectomy."

I could feel my brows shoot up to my hairline. It occurred to me, jarringly, that we'd never once talked about birth control. I was on the pill, and I knew I was clean, and Mal was, too. But then my brain digested what he was telling me, and my heart sank for him.

"That must have been a tough decision for you." I cradled his jaw when he would have dipped his head.

"It, um, wasn't really." His gaze flickered across my forehead before finally landing on my eyes. Lines of tension stood out in his neck. "I decided a long time ago that if I were ever to be a father, my children wouldn't biologically be mine." He swallowed, eyes searching. "I know we've never talked about this before, and it's a big discussion. It should probably wait for a time when we're not—"

"I don't want kids," I blurted, unable to contain the words as they spewed out of my mouth. Mal paused, considering me. I hurried on. "My career is important to me, and my life. And I don't have the greatest parental role models. There are just so many other people and things that need my attention and I'm worried I'd fuck a kid up so bad and...and maybe it's selfish, too. I like my life. I'm not sure I want to share it for the next eighteen years or whatever with someone I've never met."

I gulped, steeling myself for the look of judgement or disbelief I'd received any other time I divulged this to other people, which was rare. He gave me nothing other than that quiet examination, like he was trying to see underneath my skin.

"You're sure?"

"Yes," I nodded. The few people I'd discussed this with assured me I was just young and I'd change my mind when my "biological clock" started ticking. Well, time was still ticking and I still had zero desire to raise a child. "Trust me, I've thought about this a lot and, it might sound terrible, but it just doesn't sound like something I want."

"It doesn't sound terrible." Finally, his mouth lifted in a hint of a smile. His jaw softened underneath my fingertips. "I don't want kids, either."

"You don't? Are *you* sure?" I gasped. This was the first time anyone had ever believed me when I told them I didn't want kids. Better, this was the first time anyone had ever agreed with me.

But it was Mal. He oozed stability and structure. He'd make a top-tier father—strong and supportive, fun and flexible. He seemed like the type of guy who would want kids. "Didn't you just say if you were ever a dad, you'd adopt?"

"If. And that's a big if. It would depend entirely on what my partner wanted and what we decided we wanted together." He smiled down at me, like I was that partner. I wanted to be. Very badly. "If it were a deal breaker for the woman of my dreams, I could make it work. I just feel like my whole life is focused on serving other people. You know I love my job and helping where I can. I feel like I can do so much for this world, but I couldn't imagine coming home at the end of a long day and having to take care of other people in my free time, too."

"Yes," I whispered. I'd never been able to articulate my feelings on it so clearly. His words rang around in my chest, so right it was almost painful. Mal had always made me feel seen, special. Now, I felt understood, too. He wasn't telling me I should wait or reconsider. He got it.

Because he was right. I held people's lives in my hands every day. I held their loved ones as they cried, and had already dealt enough with other people's bowel movements to last a lifetime, without bringing an infant into the picture. I'd always known my calling was to take care of people. As long as I could remember, that hadn't included a baby. My energy, my passion, my joy...it found me elsewhere.

"Yes," he repeated, forehead pressing against mine. "And I have to say it's a relief that the woman of my dreams feels the same." Chocolate eyes gazed into mine. My heart skipped a beat.

"Oh."

"Oh." He grinned, pressing the softest kiss to my lips. "I love you. *You* are my future, too, Rija."

My eyes screwed shut, despite never wanting to look away from the adoration shining down at me from his beautiful face. "You heard that?"

"Yeah, I heard that."

"I didn't want to tell you like that," I huffed, blinking my eyes open to frown at him. As he looked at my pout, his expression softened even more, if that was possible.

"So, tell me now, Kitten."

"I love you, Mal. I love you so much sometimes I feel like I can't breathe. You're the only person I want to share my life with. And my bed, and my dog, and my sex toy collection."

He was laughing now, a big wide grin spreading across his face while he showered me with kisses. I laughed, too, kissing him back whenever he got in range of my mouth.

"I was going to tell you after this all blew over," I said, grabbing his hair and weaving my fingers through the short strands to hold him still. He kissed me again, his tongue darting between my teeth playfully.

"I've been waiting for years to tell you I loved you. I'm so glad I don't have to wait any longer."

"Years?" I'd loved Malachi for a long, long time. Maybe since the first night we'd met. I knew he liked me, sure. Was attracted to me. But love?

His smile grew. "Since the night we met, and you treated me like I'd run over your cat. You glared at me every time I tried to talk to you and I thought to myself, 'That woman who hates me, I want to spend the rest of my life with her.'"

I sputtered with laughter, trying to cover my face. I could still remember that night two years ago, when it had seemed like only righteous indignation could protect my virtue from Malachi Dobrev. I was so glad he hadn't let me hold him at arm's length for too long.

He palmed my wrists to pull them off my cheeks, kissing me again, long and hard, like he wanted to seal this moment into his memory. "You're the only one for me, Rija. You and me and Siggy. That's the family I want."

"That sounds perfect," I whispered, pressing my face into his neck. He held me like that for several minutes, rocking back and forth some more. His hand swept up and down my spine again and again. "But you know Sonnie's going to pitch a fit if she's not included in there, too."

His laugh rumbled under my shoulder. "That *does* sound perfect."

Chapter 14

Forty-eight hours locked away in an emotionally charged apartment—even one as big as the penthouse—took its toll. There was only so much doomscrolling I could do. Only so many shows we could agree on.

As the hours lurched and plodded along, I ended up fielding Mal and Sonia's bickering sibling fights more than actually watching the screen. Food was prepared, or delivered (after Asher thoroughly vetted it). We tried to sleep, and sometimes succeeded.

Asher was our constant companion, while Grayson came and went as he checked in with the new rent-a-cops down in the lobby, or did whatever it was personal security people did when an unhinged woman was running loose out there trying to murder your client.

It was a lot, but something about Asher's dry sense of humor balanced Grayson's militant rigidity, and the whole setup lulled me into a sense of dull, bored security.

I still felt the tension in the air—hard to forget when someone out there wanted us dead—but after the first day, then the second, my brain adjusted, and I just felt restless.

I'd even logged into my work laptop and caught up on patient notes and administrative paperwork, desperate for something to do other than watch Sonnie eye-fuck Asher from across the room.

We were all slumped on the couch while Asher scrolled through his phone when the piercing screech of a fire alarm shattered the quiet, lazy evening. Sonia screamed, jumping to her feet at the same time Mal jerked, lunging for me. We all looked around wildly as the high-pitched alarm blared through the apartment. My heart thundered, the wailing sharpening the cold edge of fear my brain had conveniently begun to muffle.

Asher was the only calm one, standing to place a steady hand on Sonia's back. She looked like she was ready to jump out of her skin.

"Grab your shoes," he instructed, hand cupping around his earpiece like someone was talking into it. We didn't have to be told twice. I pulled on my sneakers with shaking hands, cringing as the alarms seemed to get louder. Mal knelt to slip the leash on a yelping Siggy, before scooping him up.

"Is this for real?" Sonia shouted, pointing at the flashing alarm. Asher nodded.

"As far as we can tell. Won't know till the fire trucks get here, but I'm not taking any chances."

"We're leaving?" Mal sounded as incredulous as I felt. The walls around us felt safe. Contained. Leaving seemed like taking a big dangerous step in the wrong direction. At least, that's what the anxiety yelling at me louder than the alarms was telling me.

"I can defend a stairwell as easily as this apartment. Better, even. Bonus." His familiar crooked smile seemed out of place when every cell in my body was screaming at me to run or hide or hit something. He winked at Sonia when he pulled open the door to the emergency stairwell.

The sound of feet echoed up the floors below, bouncing off the concrete walls like thunder. More noise, more fear. I jumped about a foot in the air as Mal stepped up behind me and Siggy's trembling nose brushed my arm.

"Here's the drill." If the echoes from the stairwell were thunder, Asher's voice was the roar of the ocean, steady and calm. Rising and falling in a predictable cadence that made it easier, somehow, to focus on what he was saying. "I go first. We'll wait for the floor below us to clear then move forward. No one's coming down behind you. I'm the first one around every corner, got it?"

"Yes," I whispered, my mouth Sahara dry as he took the first steps downward. Sonia followed him close enough that she almost stepped on the back of his shoe. Even though the alarm was slightly quieter in the stairwell, the blaring rhythm set my nerves jangling, slicing straight through whatever calm I'd managed to collect today.

"Hey, Hot Asher? I appreciate how cool you seem about all this, but what if this is all some big trap or something and she's waiting for us down there?" Sonia made a decent attempt to sound normal, but her voice was shaking as hard as my knees were. As we made our way down the first flight of stairs, I clutched the handrail, so scared I could barely hold my own weight.

"You think this is our first day on the job? Gray's talking my ear off right now, clearing the basement, then he'll move on to the lobby, liaise with the emergency crews, and hopefully come hang with us for a bit. We'll secure you in one of the police cars outside, if the cops play nice. You'll watch the action, safe and sound, and then we'll come back here when it turns out there was just a wiring issue or a drill or something."

I bobbed my head, glancing back at Mal. His face was white, mouth bracketed in grim lines, but at least we were moving. We had a plan.

"Well, as long as you feel okay about it, because I'm about to pee myself." Sonia stumbled down the last step of the next flight, nearly running into Asher's back. His hand whipped out to catch her, and he looked down at her, their faces close.

"You been reading my kink journal, Beautiful Sonia?"

The laugh that cracked out of her mouth shattered some of the tension in my body. Over the alarms, I could hear Mal heave a sigh. Surely if we were in real trouble, Asher wouldn't be making sex jokes.

"Hey, that's my sister, man. Keep it clean while we're all in a confined space, alright?"

"Confined spaces. Another item on my kink list. Y'all need to stop, or it's going to get too hot in here."

More laughter rippled around us, a few of my muscles unclenching. Still, though, I couldn't help but notice while we swapped jokes and shuffled down the stairs, waiting for people to evacuate each floor before we moved forward, that Asher's body moved in a fluid, practiced prowl. He wasn't walking. He was stalking. Crouched, gun drawn, like he knew what to do with it. Even while he was putting us at ease, his body was bound by muscle memory to huddle close to the wall, padding on the balls of his feet.

I relaxed a little more every time we cleared another floor. Asher kept a constant running commentary, pulling our minds away from the fear and keeping us focused, even if it was on something ridiculous. He reported every floor we passed into his comms.

Around the fourth level, Grayson joined us, letting Asher melt silently to the back of our group to bring up the rear. Finally, the doors swung open to an empty lobby.

"Let's get you over to the trucks. Looks like there was a small electrical fire on the East side of the building. They'll have it out soon," Grayson reported.

"If they run out of water in those hoses, Sonnie Sunshine over here can help."

Sonnie whipped around to Asher so quickly, I nearly ran into her. "Shut *up!*" she shrieked.

I laughed so hard, I hardly paid attention as I crossed the courtyard and ducked into the police car. I was still laughing when it thudded shut, enclosing us in the safe, bulletproof vehicle.

***

"I'm telling Mom," Mal warned, handing me a massive glass of wine before collapsing onto the couch. Further in the apartment,

Asher and Grayson checked all the rooms and closets. The fire had been a brief and very ill-timed interval of drama. My nerves felt frayed, but we were safely ensconced in our apartment once more.

"You will not," Sonia scoffed, sipping from her own glass and fixing a plate of hummus and crackers. Seemed like it was a girl dinner type of night. I wasn't sure I'd be able to eat anything, but the appraising look Mal was giving me made me think he might force something down my throat.

"I'm just saying, you have an unreasonable amount of stories that end up with you in the back of a cop car."

She really did, and she'd been regaling us with some of her best hits for the last hour while we hunched in the police cruiser, watching the fire and police people mill around, waiting for the all clear. I knew most of the stories, even though I'd only been present for some of them. It was times like this when my mother's warnings about "that Dobrev girl" seemed to hold a bit more water.

Sonia shrugged. "They usually let me go. It's not like I end up in jail or anything."

"Except for that one time," I murmured, taking another swig. The wine felt nice on my throat. My mouth had been dry since the fire alarms went off. The liquid almost bubbled out of my mouth when I giggled at Mal and Sonia's twin reactions of horror.

"You traitor, that was a secret!"

"You went to *jail?* For *what?!*"

"Oh, come on. Even I knew about that one." Asher sauntered around the corner, snagging a carrot off Sonia's plate. "Kitchen and pantry all clear."

"Guest rooms and study clear, too. I'm going to head back down and try and corral the security. I swear, one distraction and they forget how to do their jobs." Grayson's usually stoic face twitched in a sneer as he looped Siggy's leash around his wrist. "I'll take this one for a walk before we all settle in for the night."

Sonia waited until we heard the elevator chime and the doors close before she raised her eyebrows at Asher. "I didn't think people would have the audacity to be incompetent around him."

He shrugged, grabbing another carrot before making his way to the fridge to pour a glass of water. "My brother has very particular and very high expectations. It makes him good at his job."

I whirled, the wine sloshing in my glass. "Grayson is your brother?"

"Sure is."

As Asher turned, I could see it. The green eyes weren't the exact same shade, but close. The blade of a nose, chocolate brown hair. Even with the similarities, I was caught off guard.

"He just seems so different from you," Sonia voiced what I was thinking. Grayson was so serious and focused compared to flirty, nonchalant Asher. They were polar opposites.

Asher's mouth opened to say something, but instead jerked in surprise. Then again.

Belatedly, my brain registered two cracks of a gun ringing through the apartment. A third.

Everything felt like it was underwater. I watched a cloud of blood spray out of Asher's body and onto the pristine, white marble countertops. Sonia shrieked, reaching for him, but he shoved her away, hard, before crumbling to the ground. He was saying something, yelling, as he fell, but my brain wasn't keeping up. It was fuzzy and slow and moving at warp speed at the same time.

"—go, Rija!" Suddenly, I was airborne, Mal hauling me over the back of the couch. Wine spilled in my hands, glass smashing on the floor. My vision blurred, narrowing to a pinpoint. "Run! Go!"

Bare feet scrambled to find traction on the wine-slick floor. Mal was pushing me, hauling me down the hall towards our bedroom. Like the snap of a rubber band, time sped back up again. We'd practiced this dozens of times over the last few days. If something were to happen, if she were to somehow get into the apartment... Oh, my God. Oh, my God.

She was in the apartment.

Another gunshot made me whirl to see Mal dragging Sonia into the hallway with him. In the living room, something crashed, blown apart by a stray bullet coming from the kitchen. How was she here? Where had she been hiding?

A sob burst from my throat, watching in horror, stumbling down the hall while Malachi dragged his sister after us.

She couldn't get on her feet, still struggling, still reaching for Asher. I couldn't hear him anymore.

"Mal? Baby, I'm here!" Christine's voice was shrill, manic.

Mal pushed Sonia into me, face pale. "Run."

It was a nightmare, a cruel twist of physics. I ran, but the hallway seemed endless, stretching feet into yards. Miles. My heart sped as seconds slowed. I grabbed Sonia's arm, hurtling across the floor.

The door to our bedroom was in sight. Just there, just there...

I looked back for Malachi, right on our heels. Too late.

"Don't move," Christine snarled, standing at the top of the hallway, gun pointed right at us. We all careened to a stop together, freezing at her voice and the heart-stopping metallic *click* that accompanied it.

Inches away, our bedroom door was cracked open. I caught a flash of the open closet, Siggy's empty crate, and a stray pair of shoes I hadn't put away yet. We'd been so close.

"You're with *her*?" Christine demanded, wild blue eyes swinging from me to Mal and back again. She shook her head, matted, tangled hair tumbling around her. A stench filled the air. In the YouTube video, she'd looked so normal. Now, though, nothing about her seemed right. There was a vibrating, tangible energy of wrongness emanating off her. "You knew I was coming, baby. And you're still with *her?* I came here for you!" She shouted, jerking her gun towards us. I cringed away, grabbing for Sonia.

"I'm right here, Christine. You came for me, you got me." Mal spoke in a low, soothing voice, stepping slowly in front of me and his sister. His arms were raised in surrender. Every muscle in my body seized up in denial. "Let's keep this between you and me, alright?"

"Christie," she hissed, brows squeezing over her blown pupils. "You used to call me Christie. Don't you remember?"

"Of course. Christie." I could hear the strain in his voice. Mal took another step towards her. I wanted to grab at him, snatch him back to me and safety. I must have flinched or something. Christine swerved the gun in my direction.

"Don't you fucking move, I said!" she shrieked, hands shaking. Her finger still pressed tightly on the trigger. I gulped, squeezing Sonia's hand harder. My knees felt weak. My heart was pounding so hard, I felt dizzy.

"Hey, don't worry about her. I'm right here. Let's go, let's get out of here. Just you and me," Mal soothed, taking another step forward.

"You, too!" she screamed, the tip of her gun waving back and forth between the two of us. How much more pressure would she have to put on the trigger before a bullet came flying towards us? "I love you! I did all this for *you* and you're still here with *her*? I was never good enough for you, was I?"

"Christi—"

"She doesn't know what we've been through," she screeched, spit flying in the air between her and Mal. She glared daggers at him. "You said you'd take care of me. You promised! And you *left me* just like everyone else!"

"Christine," Sonia's voice trembled as she reached a hand out to her former friend. "Please."

"*Shut. Up. You bitch!*" Christine screamed, aiming at Sonia. "If you would have just let us be together, none of this would have happened. He would be with *me*! You've been standing in my way since the beginning, I know you have. I should have killed you the second I—"

Her finger tightened on the trigger. A crack split the air, and then she was falling, the gunshot going wide, embedding into the drywall next to Sonia's head. I flinched back, blinking plaster dust out of my eyes to see Asher wrestling Christine to the ground. Malachi dove, scooping up the gun Asher had knocked free from her hand, stumbling to a stand to point it at her.

Christine was screaming, spitting and snarling, thrashing in Asher's hold while he struggled to subdue her with one arm.

"You almost killed me, you absolute cunt!" Sonia shouted, rasping. "You've terrorized my brother for years." She ripped herself out of my arms, storming down the hall.

"Sonia!" Asher jerked, raising his hand to keep her away, just as Sonia reared back to kick the other woman in the stomach. Christine used her new, prone position to her advantage, twisting to slide a gleaming knife from her boot. She swung wildly, writhing out of Asher's hold to catch Sonia in the arm with the blade. Another spray of blood splashed across the floor.

Asher kicked out, knocking Christine back and grabbing her arms, crushing her hand underneath his shoe, forcing her to drop her weapon. Mal scooped that up, too, while Asher swung her body around like it was nothing but a doll. Her face made a sickening crunch when he slammed her into the floor. Christine struggled, legs kicking, her arm bending at an awkward angle while he squeezed her throat between his forearm and bicep. One second, two. And she was limp.

He kept hold of her for another second before lowering her drooping body to the ground. Grunting, he pulled out a handful of zip ties, cinching her wrists one-handed. His other arm hung limply beside his body. Blood ran sluggishly down his sleeve.

"Do not," he glared at Sonia, who was huddled on the floor a few feet away, "approach an attacker before they are properly restrained. Yes?"

"Y-yes," Sonnie stuttered, staring at Christine while Asher looped the ties around her ankles.

"Rija." I looked at Mal, who had carefully placed the weapons to the side, out of Christine's reach. Not that she'd be able to get them if she wanted them. She was unconscious and pliant while Asher hog-tied her.

"Mal." We reached for each other at the same time. He wrapped his arms around me, burying his face in my neck. He smelled like sweat and stinging, metallic terror. I hugged him tighter as my heartbeat continued to pound in my ears, muffling everything else around us. Or maybe that was the echo of the gunshots still ringing in my head.

"Again, Sonia," Asher ordered. I pulled away to crouch beside her, Mal kneeling, too, while Asher lectured. "You do not, under any circumstances, try to kick psychopaths until I have properly restrained them. Understood? Repeat it back, because I'm not ever doing that again with you, you hear me?"

"I won't...I promise. Oh, my God, Asher." She reached for him, but he was already there, gently cradling her outstretched arm with blunt, bloodstained fingers as he examined the nasty cut that sliced down her forearm.

"Call nine-one-one," he muttered to Mal. "She'll need stitches." Mal ran to the living room to grab his phone.

"Me? Ash, *you* got shot three times. How are you still standing?" Sonia's hands rushed over his vest. It was covered in blood. He wasn't really standing, either. He'd sort of slumped down next to Sonia and didn't seem like he was planning on moving anytime soon. I reached out to take a closer look at the bullet wound on his shoulder, my training taking over even as my hands shook.

"Bulletproof vest. Protected the important stuff. Hurts like a bitch, though," Asher grunted when I applied pressure to the bullet hole in his shoulder. He was still cradling Sonia's arm with one hand, looping his earpiece in with the other. He pressed a button on his vest. "Perp is down. Two wounded in the penthouse. Repeat, perp is down. Two wounded."

"Fuck, I'm a nurse!" Sonia jerked her arm back, scrambling to undo the velcro and buckles of his vest, trying to help me put pressure on his wounds with one hand. Mal knelt beside me again, talking steadily to the emergency dispatch.

"Now you want to get my clothes off? I'm probably up for it, babe, but I might need an aspirin or something," Asher mumbled. The effect of his teasing was demolished by the waxy pallor of his skin. His lips were pale, eyes glassy as they looked up at her.

"Hey," she snapped, gently peeling back a panel of his vest. "You've been shot. No flirting while you have bullets in you."

"That's going to cramp my style more than you'd think."

In the distance, sirens wailed. Somewhere in the apartment, a door slammed.

"Asher? Ash!" Grayson barreled in, skidding to a stop at the mouth of the hallway. Siggy skidded, too, taking the corner too fast before leaping at me and Mal.

"I'm good, I'm good," Asher slurred, waving his hand. It fell, flopping into Sonia's lap. "You good? You?" He asked her, then me and Mal. Malachi reached over, pulling me close and clasping Sonnie's shoulder, dragging Siggy into his arms.

"We're good," he whispered, sliding sideways to sit down. "We're good," he repeated. Like me, maybe he needed the reassurance. I slid my hand into his, holding on tight while Sonnie and I put pressure on Asher's wounds. We listened as the sirens came closer and closer.

Chapter 15

"The alleged stalker was detained after a dramatic shootout in Dr. Dobrev's Chicago apartment. Police reports detail how despite Dobrev's private security being on the ground, Christine Malvern still managed to gain access to the building while it was being evacuated for a small electrical fire. She hid herself in the apartment's trash chute before openly firing on Dobrev and others inside."

"Trash chute," Grayson muttered, glaring at the TV. He was taking Christine's attack personally, and not just because his brother was still in the hospital.

Investigations were still ongoing, but security footage from outside our building clearly showed a figure with wild brown hair starting a fire near the air conditioning units behind the apartment. Her distraction worked, and while the firefighters were clearing the building and putting out the flames, she'd snuck in, taking advantage of the stairway doors that automatically unlocked when the fire alarms started up. She'd wedged herself into the trash chute and waited for us to return.

Asher was beside himself that he hadn't checked it.

"I have to apologize, again, on behalf of—" Grayson started, but me, Malachi, and Sonia all waved him off, interrupting and talking over him. He'd apologized enough for about three life-times.

I got the impression RISI was a legit operation, and Grayson ran a tight ship. I could tell it was killing him that Christine had ever gotten close to the apartment to begin with. While Mal didn't hold Asher or Grayson personally responsible, he'd graciously allowed RISI to install a new state-of-the-art security system in the penthouse. Grayson and another RISI team member, Aiden, were also sticking around for a few more days, providing security to deter anyone else who wanted to harm me, Dr. Do-Right, or his career.

"Investigators in the case quickly reported no evidence that Dr. Dobrev had a romantic relationship with his attacker at any point in the past, leading many to believe her claims of pregnancy were false," the reporter droned on.

"Oh, you fuckin' think?" Sonia mocked, handing cups of coffee over to me and Mal. A thick bandage hid the line of stitches running up her arm.

Mal glanced at the Keurig brew, but said nothing as he took a sip. It was progress.

I used to think my and Sonia's apartment was practically a palace, but I'd gotten used to the space of the penthouse faster than I'd thought was possible. Holing up here while the cleaning crews scrubbed blood and spackled bullet holes kind of felt like camping, now. I missed the massive multi-jet shower. Mal was jonesing for his espresso machine. Siggy was just happy to have everyone in one room, hopping from lap to lap as we sat and watched the morning news.

"Tough stuff there, Chaz," the local news anchor shook her head, her blown-out bob swaying around her face as she shook her head.

"Absolutely, Sharon. I can't imagine what the past few days have been like for Dr. Dobrev and his family. Our thoughts and prayers are with them."

"See, Mom? We have Sharon and Chaz's thoughts and prayers. We're going to be just fine," Mal grinned at where his mother was furiously crocheting in a ratan armchair across the room. Joanne and Richard Dobrev had been on a flight to Chicago the second Mal had called them to tell them about Christine's attack. They'd been crashing in the guest room slash pilates studio and hovering over us ever since the plane had landed.

I'd met them both several times, but this visit felt different for many reasons. They'd always been lovely to me, sincere and warm. Now, after I'd almost died with their children, they barreled straight into affectionate and doting territory.

I was sure it was because of Christine's attack, but I was equally sure it had something to do with Malachi telling them we were together. Joanne had given me a hug that had never seemed like it was going to end, while Richard made me a hot toddy and promptly sent me to bed as soon as my mug was empty.

"Well, I'm sure Chaz and Sharon are perfectly nice people, but I still feel like we should be closer." She glanced up from her yarn, looking at her husband for backup. Richard hummed, stroking his beard.

"I've already found a few apartments in the city that could work. Especially when I officially retire next year," Richard offered, waving his iPad in the air.

Sonia glanced back at Mal. She loved her parents, but having lived so long away from them, she was concerned they'd cramp her style if they moved to Chicago. Mal shrugged, unconcerned. I didn't help, smiling into my coffee. Maybe the parental hovering would get tiring after a while, but I couldn't say I hated it. My eyes had nearly bugged out of my head when Joanne had started talking about moving to the city "to be closer to her babies." I didn't realize parents *did that,* just packed up and moved their lives for their kids. I couldn't imagine it.

"Ma'am?" Aiden stuck his head in from the hallway. Sonia rolled her eyes, sighing.

"How many times do I have to tell you?" She slung her purse over her shoulder. He looked unrepentant as she brushed past him.

"Force of habit. Ma'am."

We could still hear her berating him after the hallway door closed. It was all in good fun. Since Sonia had barely left Asher's side since he was shot, she was getting pretty close to the RISI guys. She only came home when hospital visiting hours were over to shower and eat, and for lunch to catch up with her parents.

She'd been quiet for the last two days. Admittedly, all of us had, but she had a new, solemn aura around her that didn't feel quite right. She kept up her usual joking and inappropriate comments, but they seemed forced, like she was going through the motions instead of living in the moment.

"We'll support her however she needs. But we've all been through a trauma. It's normal to need some time to recalibrate, or reflect," Mal had told me, rubbing a soothing hand up and down my arm when I'd mentioned it to him. I grudgingly agreed, though I was keeping a close eye on both of them, just like I noticed them eyeing me over the last few days.

It still felt so surreal. Sometimes, I could blink and be right back in the hallway, the barrel of a gun pointed in my direction. Sometimes, cuddled on the couch with Mal and Siggy while Joanne worked on a cardigan for me, I felt like I'd made it all up, or it had all been a bad dream.

It didn't help that Caplan had given me the next two weeks off work to recover. Without my regular schedule and routine to ground me, everything felt off. I was in my apartment, but with Mal—always Mal, right there in touching distance, constantly Mal. Living my life, but with a personal security guard outside my door. I was still the same person I was before all this happened, but I absolutely was not.

"Dr. Dobrev, Miss Sanchez," Grayson rose, tapping his earpiece. "Just got word the penthouse is ready, if you'd like to go take a look. Make sure it's up to your standards before they pack up."

"Oh, I...so soon? That was fast, right?" I asked as Mal stood to put his coffee mug in the sink.

"Our crews work quick," Grayson shrugged. "We want you back to normal as quickly as possible. It can help, in situations like this." One more apology gift from the RISI team. Their crew of "fixers" had swept into the penthouse within hours of the shooting and had gotten to work setting everything to rights. "I can escort you, if you'd like." He nodded to the door, where Mal was already waiting.

"Oh, that's so gracious! You two go take a look. I'm sure it's just beautiful," Joanne cooed. Richard grunted, still scrolling through his real estate app, laser-focused.

I rose, not sure why my feet suddenly had such a hard time moving me across the floor. "Right now?"

Mal froze, head swinging to look at me. "Is that a problem? If you aren't up for it, Ri, I can go."

"No!" I scampered across the floor, shoving my feet into the flip-flops by the door. I might have gotten a bizarre pressure in my chest at the thought of going back up to the penthouse, but the thought of him going up there alone made me palpitate. "No," I repeated more calmly when his eyes narrowed at me. I could *feel* him sizing me up, therapy vision activated. "Let's go."

"Ri, seriously, I can go by myself."

I pulled him into the hall towards the elevators. Grayson followed a few paces behind. I was going to miss his steady presence hanging around. "No, I want to see. I just...feel..." I trailed off, finger hovering over the button for the penthouse. Malachi stood next to me, hand on the small of my back, patient. I swallowed.

"It's just a lot," I whispered, blinking away a few tears that fogged up my vision.

Mal nodded, stepping closer, like he knew I needed more support right now. "It is a lot. It's hard to move on when something like this happens. What are you feeling? Right this second?"

Oh, great. Now he was validating my feelings and asking me to name my emotions. I flopped my head to the side, resting it on his shoulder. "I have my own therapist, you know." And Dr. Peterson had been a lifesaver, booking an emergency appointment and scheduling sessions every day for the next week.

"Humor me, Kitten," Mal pressed a kiss to the top of my head, seemingly unbothered by how we were standing in the elevator with security personnel and not going anywhere. My hand dropped away from the button panel.

"I feel scared. What if being back up there makes everything come rushing back?" I whispered, looking at our reflection in the mirrored doors as they slid shut. Thankfully, no one called the elevator. We were frozen in place on my floor.

"I'm scared, too. What happened the last time we were inside those walls was horrifying. I'm terrified to relive it."

I blew out a breath. His confession made me feel a little less manic, like I wasn't totally in this alone. "And I'm sad. I loved that penthouse, and I'm worried now that it's ruined."

He grunted, pulling me closer into his chest, resting his chin on my head. "I loved it, too. I understand your concern. It might be hard to live there, after all this has happened."

We hadn't talked yet about what we would do. Part of me wanted to break my lease, run to the other side of town, and never look at this building ever again. Another part of me wanted to kick and scream at the idea. This place, that penthouse, was the first place I'd really called *home* for a long time. We'd only had a week there, but it had felt like we'd lived our whole lives in those walls. Being together, making coffee, ordering curtains…it already felt like a crucial part of my life with Mal.

"I'm angry," I whispered, tilting my head to look up at him. "I'm so pissed that she violated our space. That place was…*is* special. I hate that she might have taken it away from us."

"I know." Mal's jaw clenched. I saw the same heartbreaking mixture of grief, guilt, and rage that had haunted his face for the last two days. "I feel the same. I hate that this happened to us. To you." He hauled me closer, circling his arms around me and pressing soft kisses to my face. "The only thing we can do is try. One step at a time. For now, let's go look and see if a fresh start feels possible."

"I want a fresh start," I muttered into his chest. His fingers stroked through my hair.

"I want that, too," he sighed. "If it's a no, it's a no. I can break the lease today and have us in a new place by next week. Hell, my dad probably qualifies as a Chicago real estate expert by now."

I snorted, giving him one last squeeze before letting him go. "He has been very focused, these last few days."

"Eh, gives him something to take his mind off everything. He hides it well, but he's freaked out."

"Join the club, Richard," I murmured, looking up at Mal. He winced, and I knew he was thinking about apologizing again. He and Grayson had to cut that out. "Nope, stop that. I don't wanna hear it," I spoke over him before he had a chance to open his mouth, leaning over to key in the new security code for the penthouse. "Save that guilt for your own therapist. We're not blaming ourselves for her attacking us."

"Fair. Thank you." Mal leaned against the back wall of the elevator as we whooshed upwards. I eyed him once more in the shiny metal doors. In the other corner, Grayson leaned quietly, staring unobtrusively ahead.

"Sorry. I just needed a minute there. You probably think I'm ridiculous," I told him, watching his eyes find mine in our reflection. A smile softened his mouth from its usual hard line.

"Not at all. I was thinking how easy you two make it look. Must be nice to have someone who understands you so well."

"It is," I said simply, reaching back to where I knew Mal's hand would meet mine. My other half. My Malachi. "Do you have anyone like that in your life, Grayson?"

His brow furrowed, gaze suddenly far away as the elevator dinged and the doors rolled open. "No, ma'am. Not...right now."

It was bizarre, walking back into the penthouse. We'd only been gone for two days, and it seemed like forever. Everything was exactly the same, but it all *felt* different. Like a very real simulation that felt all too surreal. The smell of lemon cleaning products and fresh paint hung in the air. The crew hadn't just fixed the hallway, they'd scrubbed the whole place, top to bottom. As I passed by, I ran my fingers over a cashmere throw they'd meticulously folded over the back of the sectional.

Mal paced me as I moved through the space, my steps slowing the further I got. Any second now, I'd look down on the kitchen floor and see the blood stain where Asher had passed out after getting shot, before he'd roused himself to save us. I gulped, steeling myself as I rounded the island.

There was nothing there. The tiles were shiny, grout scrubbed clean. I stared, feeling a little crazy. My brain was telling me a massive pool of blood should be right there, where I'd seen it last, even though logically I knew it would be gone.

"Ri," Malachi held his hand out from where he stood at the entry to the hallway. To *the* hallway. I took his hand and let him pull me in. It was pristine. New paint, scrubbed floors. It looked better than the day Mal had moved in. The fumes felt like they were choking me. I ran my fingers across the wall, the paint dry, but still vaguely tacky beneath my fingers. No one would ever know there was a bullet lodged in the stud here. No one but us.

Mal kept hold of my hand. When I looked around again, it was like I had those blue-and-red 3D glasses on. I could see the blood. The bullet holes. And then I couldn't. They'd removed the coverings from the windows. Beyond our patio, Chicago bustled along like usual.

"We've made a few upgrades, too," Grayson murmured quietly, like he was hesitant to disturb our silent inspection. He showed us the new trash chute door he'd personally installed, with a metal plate welded to the back to stop anyone from shimmying down it again.

"Industrial grade, stainless steel frames and screws. No one's getting in the vents, either." He pointed. I didn't see anything different about the vents, but I believed him. He showed us the new alarm system, upgraded door, and window locks. "What do you think?"

He looked between Mal and I. I couldn't hold his gaze. I loved the penthouse more than I could say. They'd done a perfect job, truly incredible. But my chest hurt. Could I really keep living here, in a space that had been so utterly violated? Would I be able to move on, knowing every time I passed that spot in the hallway, the sound of a gun going off would probably ring in my ears?

"Kitten?" Mal looped his arm around my waist. "What do you think? Go or stay?"

"I'm...not sure. What do you think?"

He shrugged, looking around. "I think this feels like home to me. But I'm worried it's a little haunted."

I laughed despite the weirdness fluttering around in my stomach. That was one way to put it, yeah. *Haunted*.

"There was a delivery while you were away," Grayson pointed across the living room to a corner I hadn't looked at yet. All my attention was on the hallway. "The team didn't know where you planned to put it, so we left it there. I checked it out. It's clean."

"Not for long," Malachi whispered, grinning down at me.

The sight of the apothecary cabinet surprised another laugh out of me. I covered my mouth with my hand. After everything that had happened, my vibrator drawers were the only thing out of place.

"It really is a beautiful piece of furniture," I told Mal, walking over to run my fingers over the smooth, worn wood. The glass knobs twinkled in the sunlight. His hand joined mine, smoothing down the top, opening one of the drawers to peek inside. It was perfect. We both stood and looked at it for a beat, Grayson's big, patient presence behind us.

"We should move it," Mal said suddenly, nodding to himself. "To the bedroom, like we planned."

"You think?" My eyes ran over the piece of furniture, remembering that night in bed when he'd picked it out, when everything had seemed so bright and hopeful, like the start of something beautiful. My eyes flickered to the other side of the apartment, to the second guest room and the office we'd never fully unpacked. I wondered if the cleaners had gotten over there. I still hadn't decided how I wanted to hang Mal's diplomas. I abruptly worried that they'd gotten to it first and hung them without me.

"Yeah, let's do it." I looked up at Mal, the tiniest of smiles tugging at my lips.

The cabinet was beautiful and fucking heavy. Mal and I struggled with it for about five minutes, taking care not to scratch the floors, before Grayson decided he'd had enough and joined the fray.

I got the impression he probably could have picked up the whole thing and moved it by himself, but he humored us by letting us awkwardly fumble for handholds on the smooth surface. Navigating the hallway with three people trying to steer the massive piece of furniture was ridiculous. We stumbled into the walls more times than I could count, but finally, we set the piece down in between the two master closets. It fit perfectly.

"That's nice," Grayson commented after he'd patiently adjusted it according to my directions. An inch to the left, no, an inch over, not that way, the other way. "Drawers are small, though. What's it for?"

"Uh," I hesitated while Mal snickered behind me. "You know, this and that. Bits and bobs."

"*Bobs*," Mal hissed, trying to contain his laughter. Grayson eyed him with narrowed eyes. He knew he was missing something, but was polite enough not to pry.

I admired the drawers one last time before heading back out to the hall. As ridiculous a purpose as they served, I couldn't help the swelling in my heart when I looked at them. After everything Mal and I had been through, we were here. Our little secrets, our growing relationship, finally had a home.

I paused in the hall, my eyes drawn to the place I knew there was still a bullet buried deep behind the drywall. Bizarrely, we'd managed to scrape against the drying paint in almost the exact same spot. A smudge of brown from the cabinet's varnish marred the expanse of smooth, flat spackle and paint. I reached out to stroke the scratch, heart filling.

"What do you think, Kitten?" Mal watched as I felt up the wall. "I go where you go."

"Let's stay," I decided right then and there. I loved that little scratch more than words could describe. A reminder of our bumbling trip down the hall. Sunlight streamed through the windows, warming my back. "I want to make new memories here. Chase out the old. It won't be haunted forever, right?"

He didn't say anything, he didn't have to. His lips brushed against mine. We stood in the hallway, next to that shallow little scratch, and I knew I'd remember this kiss, this moment, forever.

Epilogue

"I hate this," I complained, flopping onto the couch.

"You'll be fine." Sonia smiled, taping up the last box to add to the massive pile by the front door. The movers would be here tomorrow to put it all in storage. "You're too caught up living the glam life with my brother in the penthouse. You've hardly missed me these past few weeks."

"That's absolutely not true, and you know it!" I sat up, irritated by her words. If anything, I missed her more than I had before Christine's attack. A week after it had all gone down, Asher had been released from the hospital, and the RISI team had returned to their home base in Atlanta. On to the next crisis, I supposed. Sonia had seemed fine when they left. Too fine. The next day, she'd packed up her own stuff and gone back to New York to finish out her travel contract there.

I worried about her every day. How was she dealing with everything? What had really gone on with her and Asher? I got the impression it was more than just a flirtation, but she hadn't spoken about him since he left. Whenever I asked if she'd heard from him, she was noncommittal, so I had no clue what was happening there.

I'd been counting the days until she came back to the city, but last week, she'd dropped the bombshell that she'd taken another travel gig, this time in Charlotte, North Carolina. She barely had a few days to come home and pack up the apartment before she started. Apparently, she had plans to make the traveling a long-term thing.

"Whatever. We both know the truth. You have a new favorite Dobrev. No time for little old me." She grinned, falling onto the couch so our legs banged together.

"Ow, you little skank, get off me. No wonder I like Mal more than you!" I shoved at her legs, still marveling at how easy it had been to integrate my relationship with Mal into my life. Despite her jokes, Sonia knew I still loved her fiercely. Life felt, strangely, perfect.

We all had our bad days. Sometimes, I'd catch Mal staring off into the distance and I knew he was reliving the horror we'd gone through. Every once in a while, Sonia FaceTimed me after work, content for me to place her on the counter or on the couch while Mal and I made dinner or watched a movie, happy just to have someone on the other end of the line. Dr. Peterson still made time for emergency appointments for me every once in a while. We all had a long way to go, but we were getting there one day at a time, just like Mal had said.

"You sure you don't want me to move my flight?" Sonia asked for the bajillionth time. I sighed, head bouncing on the back couch cushion. "Don't give me that look! You might need backup.

Someone to remind you that you have a spine, or to throw down. You know I'd love to take a few swings at your mom."

"It'll be fine." True to my promise, I'd let my parents know when the police apprehended Christine, and told them I was safe. When more details about the attack had come out in the media, they had well and truly freaked out, even going so far as to show up at our apartment a few days later when I didn't answer their calls. I hadn't even known they'd had my address. Introducing them to Joanne and Richard had been...weird.

Ever since, they'd been shockingly consistent in their outreach. Even my dad deigned to call once a week. It had taken a while for me to actually pick up. Now, though, I finally felt ready to sit down with them. We had scheduled a lunch together tomorrow to talk about our relationship. I still hadn't decided how I wanted the conversation to go, and Sonia was on edge about it.

"At least I know Mal will be around just in case," she relented, surveying the boxes. Our whole life together, the past few years, all packed away and ready for a new adventure. We had a whole box simply labeled *twinkle lights*. "This is depressing."

"You're the one who decided you didn't want to stay in Chicago anymore," I accused, poking her side as she squirmed away.

"I just...need more right now, Ri. You know?" She opened and closed her hands, as if the words she needed would fall from the sky. "You and Mal moved in together. My dad's retiring. Maybe it's the whole life-flashing-before-my-eyes moment, but I feel like I'm not doing what I'm meant to be doing, yet. I'm, like, play-acting as an adult. I need to find my life."

"Hi, I'm your whole life. Sitting right here." I waved my hand before reaching over to smoosh her face. I let her go, smoothing back some of her hair as I retreated. "I know what you mean, though. I felt like that, too, before I found nursing. I was just getting pulled along by a current, and then suddenly I felt like I had something to row toward."

"Yes!" Sonnie snapped her fingers, pointing at me. "Yes, that, minus the boat analogy, because you know ya girl don't row. But yes, you get it. You get me." Her head dropped onto the couch cushion, eyes squeezed close. "I'm going to miss you, loca."

"You too, spider monkey."

We sat together for a few more moments, quiet, soaking in the last seconds of us in this apartment together. Tomorrow, while I was at work, the movers would come to pack all of this away. By the first of next month, someone else would be on some other couch, sitting right where we were. The tape marks from the hundreds of string lights we'd crisscrossed along the ceiling would be painted over. Our epic parties in this place only a memory. We'd only been here for two years, and I'd always known it was temporary. But leaving this apartment was an end of an era. The Rija and Sonia era.

The apartment was fine, but it was her I grieved. Sure, we'd talk and text all the time, and FaceTime, and visit each other. But...that wasn't the same as living with her. I couldn't help but feel, on some level, I'd just traded one Dobrev for another. Like I wasn't allowed to have both full time.

When I'd mentioned this to Sonnie, she'd blown a raspberry in my face and told me I was being tragically dramatic, then made me paint her toenails electric blue.

When I'd repeated it to Mal, he'd pulled me into his arms and swayed back and forth, assuring me that my feelings were valid, and change could be challenging, and he was here for me, whatever I needed. After a while, when I'd calmed down, he tucked some hair behind my ear, leaned down, and whispered, "There can only be one," then laughed hysterically while I beat him with a throw pillow.

"Come on, let's go see what my stupid brother is up to." Sonia heaved to her feet, pulling me up with her. We both took one last look at the apartment before we closed the door and headed to the elevators.

Maybe it was just a fact of life that I couldn't have my best friend and my boyfriend at the same time. I'd have to learn to take Sonia in smaller doses—long distance and only during special occasions. I'd done that once with Mal, hadn't I? And now I couldn't imagine a world where I woke up without him next to me, Siggy sneaking in between us for an unsanctioned cuddle.

"I'm glad you two finally came to your senses. Thank God for me." Sonia loved to take credit for our relationship, blatantly ignoring me anytime I tried to tell her that Mal and I had been *a thing*, even unofficially, for months before her meddling. Even with her leaving, and how awful it was going to feel to learn to live without her long-term, I was forever grateful to my friend for understanding my relationship with her brother.

"You're welcome for this, too," she muttered, giving me a cryptic smile as the doors slid open to the penthouse. I shuffled away, not trusting the sneaky gleam in her eye. I was so wary it took me a second to notice the candles lining the foyer and hallway.

"What?" I asked, peering out at the tea lights flickering in the dim apartment.

"Go see," Sonnie whispered, pushing me out of the elevator. She smiled when I looked back at her, blowing me a kiss and waving me forward.

I nearly stumbled, staring at all the candles. There had to be dozens charting a pathway from the elevator to the living room. When the living room came into view, I mentally recalibrated my math. There weren't just dozens, there were *hundreds*. Tiny lights danced on nearly every available surface. What wasn't covered in candles held massive vases of fresh flowers. It smelled like a garden center.

And there, in the middle of it all, was Malachi, standing in one of his tuxes. At his feet, Siggy sat perfectly still, sporting his own little bowtie. The only movement from my favorite dog in the world was his wildly thumping tail.

"Mal?" I wasn't sure what question to ask. What was going on? Was this what I thought it was? Was he trying to burn our apartment down? At the sound of my voice, Siggy hopped up to all four paws.

"Sigmund," Mal warned. "We practiced this. Sit." The dog obediently sat on his haunches, looking up at Malachi, who offered him a treat from his pocket before looking up at me. "Hi, Kitten."

"Hi, Honey. Quite a welcome home."

Mal nodded, looking around at his handiwork. He must have been setting this up for hours, the whole time I'd been downstairs helping Sonia pack. He'd told me he had work calls. What a stinker.

"It's a good ambiance," he agreed, his gaze drawing back to me like it was magnetized. My heart fluttered in my chest. His face in the candlelight, with that soft, adoring expression, was almost more than I could handle.

"Yeah, it is." I swallowed, watching him stand perfectly calm in the middle of our beautiful living room. The home we'd built, were re-building, together. "What the hell is going on?"

"I could have done a really great speech telling you how much I love you and the life we have together, but you already know that." He quirked an eyebrow. I didn't deny it. He told me every day, both aloud and through all the little things he did for me, how much he loved me. "I thought about some very epic, emotional proclamations telling you how you're the only woman I've ever truly loved and the other half of my soul and all that. But every time I started practicing, my throat got a little tight, and I didn't think that was a good idea."

He gave a little cough, sounding like his vocal chords were squeezing, regardless. Mine were rapidly constricting, my pulse hammering harder and harder.

"Mal—"

"But really, I've been waiting to do this for a while and I thought at the end of the day I should just make it simple." Mal squared his shoulders, looking me in the eye. "You said you wanted to make new, good memories here, Rija. I'm really hoping this makes your list."

He lowered down to one knee, pulling a velvet box from his jacket pocket. My hands flew to my mouth, tears already forming in my eyes. My answer already forming on my lips.

"Rija," Mal paused, glancing down at Siggy. "Sig, kneel," he hissed. My puppy lowered into a little play bow. My poor heart couldn't take this level of surprise and cuteness and joy. I laughed as tears started rolling down my cheeks.

"Rija," he began again, looking back up at me with shining eyes. "Will you make me and Siggy the happiest creatures on the face of the earth? Will you marry me?"

A happy sob wracked my shoulders. "Cariño," I reached for him. He stood immediately, crossing the polished floor to me. Siggy close on his heels. I grabbed at his arms. "It's only been two months."

"Kitten, it's been two years. I would have dropped down on one knee in your kitchen during Cinco De Mayo if I hadn't thought you'd chase me off with a butcher knife." His hands swept my face, wiping the tears away. "Say yes," he whispered. "Please."

"Say yes!" Sonia shouted from somewhere behind me.

"Yes! Obviously yes! Yes, times infinity. Yes, forever. Every single day, yes," I pulled him into my arms, bawling my eyes out and clinging to the best man I'd ever had the pleasure of knowing. He sighed against me, relief pouring out of him. He squeezed me tighter.

"I love you."

"I love you, too!" I hiccuped, pulling back to plant kisses wherever I could reach on his face. Siggy picked up on the happiness of the moment, jumping up to his hind legs to paw at us. Mal scooped him up and gathered us close. Our family.

A champagne cork popped behind me. Sonia poured three flutes that were already waiting on the counter.

"You knew?" I smiled and accused and wept and laughed all at the same time. She scoffed at me, joining our group hug after pressing a glass into my hand.

"Obviously, I knew. I told him he should do it today."

"Not true, I told *her* I wanted to do it before she left for wherever the hell she's going to now," Mal countered, glaring while he snagged a glass from her. Sonia rolled her eyes.

"Show her the ring, you dummy."

"Fuck." Mal shoved the glass back at Sonia, pulling back to open the velvet box he'd been holding. A gorgeous emerald-cut diamond winked out at me, framed by a delicate, twisting platinum band. I couldn't stop the new wave of tears that tumbled down to my chin.

"Oh, no, she hates it," Sonia gasped, grinning. I loved it and she *knew* I loved it since she'd been privy to my nursing school Pinterest board era and had access to every dream wedding board I'd ever created, where emerald-cut diamonds featured prominently.

"You helped him pick out the ring?" I sounded watery, pulling them both back to me for a group hug. Siggy wiggled around our legs.

"Don't lie," Mal warned, smoothing his hand up and down my spine and pressing soft kisses against my neck. Sonia huffed.

"Mal picked out a few. I approved of this one."

"I did, too," Mal bickered back. Sonia clicked her tongue and eased out of our embrace, giving us some space. Mal scooped me up, sliding the ring onto my finger. It fit. I was still crying so much that I could barely see what it looked like against my hand. I got the impression that it was absolutely perfect.

"Our reservations are at seven, people. You have limited lovey-dovey, gooey staring time. Start now. You'd better be dressed when I come back up here!" Sonia drained her glass, pausing to wrap her arm around my neck and press a smacking kiss to my cheek. "Congrats, sis," she whispered, before sashaying down the hall toward the elevator.

"Reservations?" I tilted my chin to rest on Mal's chest. The backs of his fingers stroked stray tears away from my cheeks.

"La Belle Vie. Private room." He named one of the swankier restaurants in the city, trailing kisses wherever his fingers touched.

"Fancy," I replied just before his tongue swept into my mouth. My body sparked and fizzed like the wine in my hand. I cupped his jaw, feeling the unfamiliar weight of the ring against my skin. He groaned when I flicked my tongue across his bottom lip. "I should change, then," I whispered, nipping my teeth along his freshly shaved jaw.

"You're perfect," he ducked, capturing my mouth again. He eased his hands under my shirt, stroking the skin of my back.

"I'm wearing sweatpants," I gasped, arching into his touch. Even months later, the slightest press of his skin against mine was enough to light me up. I was still absolutely starving for him.

"If you want to get out of them, I have a fun activity for you." He placed one last stinging, lingering kiss against my lips before leaning over to pull something out of the couch cushions. "Didn't feel right to open this one in front of my sister."

I'd never seen the box before, but I was familiar with the shape. Long, rectangular. I pulled on the silky white ribbon to reveal the white vibrator, decorated with little shining crystals all along the bottom. I barked out a laugh.

"You bought me a proposal vibrator?"

Mal grinned down at it like it was a treasure. "Have to hit all the big milestones, Kitten."

"Mmhmm. Didn't you say something once about having your cake and eating it, too?"

"Exactly." Mal's smile turned wicked as he reached down to pluck the toy out of the box. "I estimate we have twenty minutes before Sonia comes barging back up here." He scanned my body, looking at me like I was wearing lingerie instead of dusty moving clothes. "How fast you think you can make yourself come?"

"Depends," I purred, grabbing the vibrator, my ring sparkling in the candlelight. "How long can you keep your hands to yourself?" I pulled off my oversized t-shirt, leaving me in a black sports bra and gray sweatpants that hung low on my hips. *His* sweatpants. Mal swallowed.

"Not long." He was already reaching for me, even as I backed away down the hallway to our bedroom. My champagne glass clicked on the countertop as I set it down. Mal followed, looking like he was not in control of his own actions.

I held his gaze as I flicked the toy on, buzzing filling the air between us. I gripped it as if it were his shaft, pumping my fist up and down, making sure he saw my ring flash with my hand's motion. He groaned. I grinned.

Two months ago, I could never have imagined this would be my reality. I had hardly dared to think of a world where Mal and I would use these toys not for proxy, but for fun. I could never have dreamed of how perfectly our life with Sonia and Siggy and this apartment and his new clinic would come together.

Yes, we had gone through hell to get here, but on the other side, life looked sweet.

"You said something about making more good memories here. Maybe you can help me make another?"

He lunged, grabbing the toy out of my hands and scooping me up in one arm. I laughed all the way down the hall. He kicked the door shut behind us.

Also by Julia Fisher

 *She's mastered the heart's anatomy, just not its emotions.*

Doctor Lainey Carmichael doesn't have time for relationships. She's too focused on finishing her prestigious cardiothoracic surgery fellowship and landing her dream job. Besides, all the men she knows are doctors, and she's sworn never to date anyone from work (again). But an unexpected confession from her quiet, burly, kind-of-boss, Dr. Samuel Reese, makes her take notice of something other than her scalpel.

While Sam's covert attraction to Lainey has only grown over the years, she hardly noticed he existed. Now, as he captures her attention again and again, he might have a chance to prove he's more than just another attending.

The good news? They've got more chemistry than a pharmaceuticals lab. The bad news? Lainey, herself, might be the biggest obstacle in the way of her own happiness.

Hearts on the Table is a standalone coworkers-to-lovers romantic comedy with a dirty-talking, cinnamon roll
MMC and a charming, whip-smart FMC with work-life-balance issues. For fans of strong women who
can have it all, and the men who love them. Found family, secret/forbidden relationship, and a little
biting.

Read Hearts on the Table now!

About the author

Romance author Julia Fisher writes about smart, relatable characters, sizzling chemistry, and life-changing love stories. She lives in Atlanta with her family, too many pets and a massive TBR she'll never be able to work through.

Acknowledgements

As always, a massive thank you to my alpha readers, who helped me craft this word clay into one of the funnest stories I've ever written. (Yeah, I said funnest.)

This novella would not have been possible without Houston's tactical guidance. You da real one.

And of course, for everyone who gave Hearts on the Table a shot, and continues to give this fledgling author your time and attention. Thank you, thank you, thank you.